INVISIBLE FRIENDS

DOUG SIMPSON

Copyright (C) 2021 Doug Simpson

Layout design and Copyright (C) 2021 by Next Chapter

Published 2021 by Magnum Opus– A Next Chapter Imprint

Edited by Fading Street Services

Cover art by CoverMint

This book is a work of fiction. Names, characters, places, and incidents are the product of the author's imagination or are used fictitiously. Any resemblance to actual events, locales, or persons, living or dead, is purely coincidental.

All rights reserved. No part of this book may be reproduced or transmitted in any form or by any means, electronic or mechanical, including photocopying, recording, or by any information storage and retrieval system, without the author's permission.

Invisible Friends is dedicated to all of the parents of children with imaginary friends.
Are you really sure they are imaginary?

A big thank you goes out to all of the hard-working staff at my publisher, Next Chapter. You are priceless and precious. Thank you for all you do for us.

1

"Hello."

"Hi Dacque, it's Dani. This will be brief, and I cannot talk very loudly. A friend here at the law office confided in me during our lunch break that she is beginning to suspect her six-year-old daughter's imaginary friend may in fact not be imaginary after all. She knows a little about our interest in souls and reincarnation, and I suggested she needs to talk with you. Any chance that you can meet us after five in the parking garage down the street from our office, or alternatively outside of our building, and we can walk together to the parking garage so the three of us can huddle in a car for a private chat?"

"Sure, Dani. That will work. I will be waiting outside of your office building before five."

"Great. Thank you. See you then. Bye for now."

"Bye."

2

Dacque was people watching outside of The Murtagh Building by ten minutes before five, and the ladies accompanied the departing throngs through the revolving doors at five minutes after five.

"Connie, I would like you to meet a very special friend of ours, Dacque LaRose," Dani said when they stopped in front of Dacque.

"Dacque, this is Connie Cantland, the friend I told you about earlier with the six-year-old daughter."

They shook hands and proceeded down the street to the parking garage in silence. The first of their vehicles they came upon was Connie's Jeep Patriot, so it became the default choice for their secret conversation. Dani quickly hopped into the back seat to leave the passenger seat open for Dacque in order to facilitate his anticipated conversation with Connie.

"Dani told me on the phone earlier that you are becoming skeptical about your daughter's supposedly imaginary friend actually being imaginary," Dacque said to Connie after the three of them were seated comfortably inside the Patriot.

Connie chuckled. "I know it is common for youngsters to

have imaginary friends but Camille, or Cammi as we usually call her, seems to know things about her imaginary friend that normal six-year-olds would not likely to be able to make up. Dani told me earlier that you have seen, talked to, and even worked with spirits or souls in the past. Does that include imaginary friends?"

"Well, I cannot say that I have ever been called upon to deal with a child's imaginary friend, but I did assist five earthbound souls or spirits, stranded at the Anywhere Children's Hospital, to cross over and join their eagerly-awaiting relatives."

Connie smiled. "That sounds close enough for me. So, what do I or we do now?"

"I think the first thing we should do is for me to have a little chat with Cammi so that I understand how much she knows about her little friend. Not alone, of course, but with you and your husband present as well. Can you set that up whenever it is convenient?"

"I think the first thing that I need to take care of is to bring my husband up to date. He knows that I am not sure Cammi's little friend is actually imaginary, but he knows nothing about you and your knowledge concerning souls and spirits. Dani has told me a little bit about what she knows on the subject, but it would probably be wise for you to meet with Carson and I before you meet with Cammi, so we have a little better understanding of what you think might be going on in our home."

"I agree." Dacque removed a card from his wallet and handed it to Connie. "When you and Carson are ready for a chat, give me a call and we can set something up. I am retired so my schedule is usually pretty unencumbered."

"Thank you, I will do that," Connie replied and tucked Dacque's card in her purse.

3

Connie had Cammi bathed and into bed by eight o'clock and hesitantly but determinedly brought Carson up to date on her earlier conversations with Dani and Dacque. Carson thought the whole idea of survival of souls and reincarnation was humorous, if not outright absurd, but Connie stubbornly hounded him to listen to her suspicions concerning their daughter's imaginary friend. She advised him that she would have Dacque over the first evening he went out with his buddies if he did not agree to be present when Dacque arrived. A somewhat upset Carson told his unwavering wife to telephone Dacque right then and there and see if he was willing to come over immediately to take care of this anticipated, irritating meeting.

DACQUE DROVE into the Cantland's driveway within fifteen minutes. Connie offered him refreshments, which were declined, and the threesome settled down in the family room.

"As Carson does not know much about souls and reincarnation, and to be honest I likely do not know much more than he does," Connie started things off to get their conversation underway and hopefully prevent Carson from saying anything nasty, "maybe the best way to get us rolling along here would be for you to share with us your experiences with spirits or souls and if you like, reincarnation, if that is alright with you, Dacque?"

"I think that is the perfect way to begin. My wife passed away from cancer over ten years ago now, and not too long after she left us some unexplainable events began to occur in our house. They culminated one evening when I was sitting in our living room reading a book. I looked up for some reason and sitting there in her favorite chair across the room was my beautiful wife. She looked more like she did back when she was thirty than when she passed on. This is not unusual, and I can explain that later if you like but for now, I will continue with the story. My wife smiled at me and then said something like, 'I am fine. There is no more pain. You must stop moping around and get on with your life.' She then faded away and as far as I know never returned. The strange events that were occurring around the house also ceased.

"That took place up in Canton, Ohio, where we had basically spent our entire lives. Before long, I decided to sell our home there and move south before the harsh weather set in. I rented an apartment here in the city of Anywhere for the winter. I did not necessarily plan to remain here, but I liked it so much I never bothered to move elsewhere.

"After the visit from my wife's soul or spirit, and before I decided to sell our home, I searched out a book I had read years earlier about reincarnation and the survival of souls. It is called There Is a River, by Thomas Sugrue, and it is the story of this amazing man named Edgar Cayce who could put himself in a deep, self-induced hypnotic trance state and perform miracles while he was under. I have a copy of his book for you out in my car, but I decided to not bring it in with me until I saw how you folks received my information.

"A couple of years after I moved here to Anywhere, I came across a group called the Reincarnation Enlightenment Group. It was started by and is still run by a licensed Regression Therapist who also has a keen interest in investigating incidents of suspected reincarnation. She will give her group members past-life regressions in her spare time for free as part of her research into reincarnation. I have had three regression sessions with her and uncovered about ten of my past lives. Enough about that for now.

"As my understanding of souls and reincarnation increased, I gradually realized that I was apparently receiving messages from the other side, or from the Heavenly Powers if you prefer the term. Once I actually accepted that I was being sent messages, I consciously attempted to pay more attention to these messages than I had ever bothered to do before. Many people probably receive messages which they attribute to intuition and pay little or no attention to them, but the secret is to pay attention. The more I paid attention, the more messages I seemed to receive, which I guess makes good sense.

"The next startling development in all of this was that the Heavenly Powers began asking me to help them with assisting people in need, not necessarily financially but to help them to get through some difficult times. Dani Christian, Connie's co-worker, was one of the first people I was asked to help," Dacque said, looking directly at Carson. "Dani's problem was not a very significant one, but I suppose that also makes good sense. If the Heavenly Powers were breaking me in to be part of their assistance assignment program, then they would not start me off with a whopper of a problem, now would they?"

Carson smiled and Connie responded. "That makes perfect sense."

"Good. Continuing then, my next assignment after helping

Dani get her life back on track, turned out to be a whopper of a one that I was afraid was way over my head. It started with a dream about a girl apparently dying at Anywhere Children's Hospital many years ago. I never saw any date, but I thought the clothing in the dream was from sixty or seventy years ago. I was also given her name. I never bothered to search out the name right away as I had not been given any directions as to what I was expected to do.

"That didn't last long. The very next morning, on my usual morning walk around the city, I was ordered by my now occasional little voice in my ear or head to go into the Anywhere Children's Hospital, as I was walking by it. No directions on what I was supposed to do when I got in there, just to go in. To make a long story short, I became a volunteer at the Hospital and was eventually led to the earthbound spirit of the deceased girl in my dream. The only problem was she had four spirits of even younger children that she was taking care of like a big sister would. I eventually managed to get all five of them to crossover and join their eagerly awaiting relatives.

"A marvelous bonus from this assignment is that I acquired a lovely lady friend who is a widow and is still a nurse at the hospital. She also saw all five of the stranded spirits and was with me when they all crossed over which actually took place on two different occasions. It is likely that I will need to work with Cammi's little spirit friend in a similar fashion as I did with the spirits of these five children at the hospital.

"I have also encountered one more spirit, but this spirit is not earthbound like the children were. It was the spirit of an acquaintance of mine who was viciously murdered. His spirit wanted me to assist it to find its murderer. That is also a very interesting story but has little relevance to Cammi's visitor. I am also pretty sure that my wife's spirit was not earthbound but visited me only to get me out of my grieving funk. And that is my story concerning spirit visitors. I welcome your questions or comments."

Connie glanced over at Carson, having absolutely no idea what he thought about Dacque's story explaining his spiritual journey. He returned her glance and then turned back towards Dacque. "You mentioned a book earlier about this Cayce chap. I think I would like to read that book if it is alright with you. I must admit that it is difficult for me to grasp how all of this would work, not that I am doubting your word, let me make that perfectly clear, but I need to get a better understanding of all of this."

"I brought it along, hoping I would hear those words but did not bring it inside in case it caused either of you to feel like I was jamming it down your throat. I actually have two somewhat similar books out in the car so that each of you can read one and then switch them around if you wish. Let me go and retrieve them."

Dacque returned in a couple of minutes with the two books. He handed Thomas Sugrue's, There is a River, to Carson, and then turned his attention to Connie. "This second book has a lot of similarities to the first one but is much more modern. It is a true story of how a renowned Miami Psychiatrist, Dr. Brian L. Weiss, got introduced to reincarnation by one of his deeply hypnotized patients. I am sure you will enjoy it too," he said and handed her the book. "I would suggest that both of you read both books and give me another call when or if you would like to have a second get-together."

Connie and Carson thanked Dacque profusely for taking his time to enlighten them on his educational experiences and walked him to the door.

4

It was a week later before Connie telephoned Dacque again.

"Hello."

"Hello, Dacque, it's Connie. I hope I am not disturbing you?"

"Not at all. How is it going?"

"Good. Carson and I have each read the two books you left with us and we now have a much better understanding of souls and their reincarnation. We agree that we should ask you to check into Cammi's little friend and hopefully determine whether it is possible for her association with him to be in any way harmful to her. She told us his name is Zianos, if I heard her correctly, but he asked her to just call him Zee. Are you still willing to get involved with our little problem?"

"Of course. I thoroughly enjoy the challenge of meeting and talking with spirits and helping them out in any way possible."

"Great. What is our next move?"

"I need to get to know Cammi first and gain her trust. It is unlikely that Zee would appear to me no matter how much time I spent in Cammi's room unless she sort of introduces me to him as her mother's friend."

"That makes sense. When would you like to meet Cammi?"

"I would like you to coach Cammi for a while on your desire to know more about Zee and to have her introduce me to Zee because I am very interested in meeting him, too. As young as she is, it will be really important to our mission to make sure she is genuinely comfortable in my presence, and probably in my presence in her room without you and your husband there with us. That also means that you and your husband must become perfectly comfortable with me being alone with her in her bedroom, possibly sometimes for hours at a time. I do not know anything about them, but I understand people can rent or purchase these child security cameras to keep a check on their small children, and also their babysitters at times as well. I assume you would likely be able to watch a monitor in your living room or on your computer whenever Cammi and I were in her room waiting for Zee to join us. I have no idea whether Zee will actually appear on one of those cameras but Cammi and I certainly will. It is just something you might want to think about."

"Wow! This is not going to be simple, is it?"

Dacque chuckled. "Not very simple, I will admit."

"Okay, thanks Dacque for your time and advice. I will bring Carson up to date on the things we need to do and get back to you. Have a good rest of your evening."

"Thank you and you also."

5

Another week passed before Dacque heard back from Connie.

"Hi Dacque. Sorry it has been so long between phone calls. We have been having a little trouble getting Cammi to meet with you. We have tried telling her that you are really interested in meeting Zee, but she is quite shy by nature, so she has little interest in meeting some strange man. Carson and I think our best shot here would be for you to visit with us on a regular basis without even talking about Zee, so that Cammi gets accustomed to having you in the house and no longer thinks of you as some stranger. What do you think?"

"That sounds like a good idea. What kind of things is she interested in when it comes to games or books or sweets? It may help if she gets used to me bringing her something each time I visit, or all of us playing her favorite games with her."

"I like that idea. Just skip the treats. We are trying to keep those to a minimum around here. She loves books, and we have lots of games she likes to play. When would you like to start this process?"

"Like I told you in your Jeep that day we first met, I am

retired, and my schedule is generally pretty flexible. I am sure you and Carson have many more restrictions on your time than I do so you pick the days and times, and I am sure I will have very few conflicts, okay?"

"Okay, that's great. How does Saturday afternoon sound for starters? I think that will work for us if it works for you, but I will confirm it with you Friday evening if that sounds alright?"

"That sounds just fine."

"Great. Talk to you on Friday. Thank you."

"You are welcome."

6

Dacque's telephone rang at eight-thirty on Saturday morning. He did not have caller ID but he knew exactly who would be on the other end of the line.
"Good morning."
"Good morning, Dacque, it's Dani. It is a beautiful day out there, so I suspect you are going for your morning walk soon?"
"Definitely. Are you joining me?"
"Yes. MacDunnah Park, our bench?"
"Of course. When are you leaving?"
"Anytime you like."
"I'm ready now, how about you?"
"I'm ready. See you there."
"Bye."
Dacque tried to walk every morning, weather permitting, right after breakfast. Sunday is an exception. If he is walking alone, he has his established walking routine that involves heading north one day and south the next. After leaving his apartment he allows the stoplights and stop signs to determine his journey as his main goal is to not stop walking on the outward route. On occasion he has stubbornly circled the same

block a time or two in order to achieve his objective of not halting on his outward walk. On his way back home, he no longer needs to worry about fulfilling his daily exercise quota and sometimes does some shopping if needed. He is no longer concerned about stopping at stoplights and stop signs.

MacDunnah Park, and what they affectionately call 'our bench', is where his little voice directed him to a sobbing, unemployed Dani Christian on one of his earliest rescue projects. Even though Dacque is old enough to be Dani's grandfather, they have become close friends and are often Saturday morning walking partners if Dani is available to join him.

7

At the sound of the doorbell, Connie walked towards the front door and Carson took off in search of Cammi. "Good afternoon, Dacque. Thank you for joining us today."

"It is my pleasure, believe me."

As Connie and Dacque strolled into the living room from the foyer, Carson and Cammi appeared from the opposite direction. "Here they are. Dacque, I would like you to meet our daughter, Cammi. Cammi, please say hello to Mr. LaRose."

"Hello, Mr. LaRose," Cammi said in a voice barely above a whisper as she centered her attention more on the package wrapped in red paper in the left hand of her visitor.

"Hello, Cammi. I am very pleased to meet you. Your mom mentioned the other day that you loved to read books, and when I came across one that I was sure you would like I just had to bring it here to you today." Dacque handed the parcel to a now-grinning Cammi.

"And what are the magic words?" Connie asked quietly.

"Thank you, Mr. LaRose. Can I open it, Mommy?"

"Of course. It is for you."

Cammi quickly attacked the wrapping paper, tucking it under her arm to free up both hands to have a good look at the book's cover. Her grin was priceless.

"What is it called?" Connie asked.

"Ro...Rosa...Rosabelle Rides a Reindeer."

"Very good, honey. You probably have never seen the name Rosabelle before."

"Would you like to read the story to me, Cammi, or maybe I could read it to you if you prefer?" Dacque inquired.

Cammi opened the book at random and glanced at a page. "There are some hard words in there that I do not know," she said and handed the book to Dacque.

Dacque glanced at Connie who nodded her head towards the sofa. Dacque sat down near one end. "Would you like to sit up next to me so you can see the pictures as I read the story?" he asked Cammi.

She did not move and looked over at her mother.

"Go ahead, honey. Daddy and I will sit here too because we want to listen to the story as well."

Cammi climbed up on the sofa and settled in fairly close but not too close to Dacque.

"Rosabelle Rides a Reindeer," Dacque read from the cover. "Have you ever ridden a reindeer, Cammi?" he asked, looking at the precious bundle next to him.

"No," she replied with a giggle. "I have never even seen a real reindeer. Have you?"

Dacque had to stop and think about that for a minute. "You know something, Cammi, I don't think that I have ever seen a real reindeer either. I have seen lots of deer when I lived up north in Ohio and they would be kind of cousins to the reindeer, just like there are many different kinds of dogs, but I have never seen a real reindeer like Santa Claus has up in the North Pole."

Dacque proceeded to read the story to his attentive

audience. "Well, Cammi, did you like the story?"

"Oh, yes. Very much."

"I am glad to hear that," Dacque replied and handed the book to Cammi.

She hopped off of the sofa. "Can I put it on the bookshelf in my bedroom and then go back to playing with my toys, Mommy?"

"Sure, honey, but first what do you say to Mr. LaRose?"

"Thank you, Mr. LaRose for the nice book and for reading it to me today," she said and ran off towards the rear of the house.

"That went well I think," Connie commented after Cammi was out of range.

"I think so too," Dacque responded. "We will take this one step at a time and I hope she will eventually feel comfortable with me around. I never had much of an opportunity to spoil my grandchildren as they all live many hundreds of miles away, but I volunteer a morning or two a week at the Anywhere Children's Hospital and spend a lot of time with youngsters Cammi's age, reading them stories and playing games with them."

"That is a very nice thing for you to do. Changing the subject on you, now that Carson and I have both read the Edgar Cayce and Dr. Weiss books you were nice enough to bring to us, we think we might be interested in investigating our past lives like you and Dani have done."

"That is wonderful news," Dacque commented.

"You told us earlier about the reincarnation group that you and Dani belong to and the regression therapist who runs it but nothing concerning how we join the group. How does that work?"

"It is pretty simple. I can recommend you for membership which makes it easier than a total stranger requesting entry. You need to select an alias that you will use within the group. It helps to protect everyone's identity from other members. There has never been a problem within the group but there is always the possibility someone could ask for admission for reasons beyond their research into reincarnation. You also need an email account other than your commonly used email account, basically for the same reason of ID protection. We do not need some spammer having access to our main email addresses. Membership is free."

"That's not a big problem, just a little work," Connie commented. "What kind of alias do we need?"

"There are over a hundred members, but it is not difficult to pick an alias that nobody else has selected. Mine is Streetwalker, Dani's is Beanpole, a nickname her brother blessed her with when she would not stop growing as a teenager one summer. The regression therapist uses Eyeonthepast. I can leave it with you to think about for a while if you like, or we can work on it now if you think you are ready to give this a shot. Those of us who are personal friends or associates know each other's alias. All members receive a list of all members' aliases and their special email addresses, but of course not their real names."

"What do you think?" Connie asked Carson.

"I guess we can do it now. Joining up does not mean we have to rush right into a regression session, I assume?"

"Of course not. I think all of the people that I have encouraged to join have actually gone on to request a regression session, but I probably only personally know ten or fifteen percent of the membership. They used to hold a monthly members' meeting but poor attendance has caused Eyeonthepast to skip some of those so they may be approaching extinction. Do the two of you have a second, little-used email account or do you need to apply for one?"

"I have one I can use," Connie said.

"So do I," Carson added.

"Great. Any ideas about an alias you would like to use?"

"I can us Cantdoit," Carson said.

"I think I will go with Cancan," Connie chimed in.

"Great, please write your email addresses and aliases on a piece of paper for me and I will email Eyeonthepast with the information when I get home, along with my recommendation that you be accepted. You should receive an email from her within a few days with your membership confirmation, a list of aliases and email addresses, along with some membership rules, primarily the requirement of secrecy when you know the real ID of some members like we do. After that you can request a regression session whenever you are ready. Eye, as we often call her, will usually do sessions on Saturday mornings, and may also do some Saturday afternoons, Sundays, and evenings but those are at her discretion. I should mention the location problem while I am thinking of it. Eye does not hold the group's regression sessions in her office because that would reveal her identity. Members must provide a location for their session. Many of the homeowners like you are also reluctant to hold them in their own homes for the same reason. I offer everyone that I recommend for membership the option of holding their regression sessions in my apartment. Many people take me up on it, so you are welcome to do the same."

"Great, thank you for everything that you are doing for us, and we are basically total strangers," Connie said.

"You are most welcome. Since Dani recommends you that is all that I need to know. By the way, I walked with Dani this morning, as we often do on Saturday mornings, in MacDunnah Park. Is there anything else we should discuss today before I leave you folks to enjoy the rest of your weekend?"

Connie and Carson looked at each other and shook their heads. "It looks like that is all we can take care of for today, but we have certainly accomplished a lot this afternoon," Connie said. "Thank you again for everything and before you depart, I will get a piece of paper for you with our email addresses and aliases."

8

Dacque's telephone rang just after seven on Tuesday evening. "Hello."

"Good evening, Dacque, it's Connie. I wanted you to know that Carson and I both received our confirmation emails today from Eyeonthepast for our membership in the Reincarnation Enlightenment Group."

"That is great news. Thank you for telling me."

"You are welcome. I am becoming more and more interested in experiencing a past life regression session and I am curious how long the waiting list usually is before Eye could get to me?"

"Apparently it varies widely. It is still early in the week and there may be a good chance she can fit you in this Saturday. You now have Eye's email address so send her off a request for a spot this Saturday if one is available, or if you are available, on the next Saturday if this week her schedule is already filled up. Are you going to have your session in my apartment?"

"If you are sure you do not mind, that would be wonderful, thank you."

"That is no problem. Eye has been here so many times she can probably find it with her eyes closed."

"Don't you usually walk with Dani on Saturday mornings?"

"Pretty regularly, yes, but that presents no problems. We can just walk around the street here near my place."

"You won't be present during my regression session?"

"No. Eye considers everyone's past life information personal and confidential, so she does not allow witnesses. She does record each session, or actually each of the individual past lives uncovered during the session, but at the conclusion of the session she gives the CDs to the reading recipient. She also does not like us to reveal the details from our uncovered past lives with anyone else, unless both individuals shared an incarnation together and they both know about it, not just one of them. For example, you cannot tell Carson or Dani any details from your past lives unless you identify them as being incarnated back then with you and they also have uncovered that same incarnation.

"This is important because Carson has not yet had a past life regression, so even though you know you were previously incarnated together you must keep the details a secret until he also discovers that same past life. On the other hand, if you uncover a past life with Dani then you can ask her if she uncovered an incarnation in, for example Paris, and if she says yes then try to establish whether you are both referring to the same time frame. Dani could have had two incarnations in Paris four hundred years apart so you may not be thinking the same incarnation at all. If Dani did not know you at the time of her regression session, then she could not have identified you at that time.

"I have had that problem often with people I have recently become acquainted with long after I had my regression sessions. If I did not know them then, I could not identify them, but when they uncovered our lifetime together later, they could identify me. I know that is somewhat long and wordy, but do you understand?"

"I think so. We can only share our past life information with those who also experienced a past life with us and they are also aware of that past life, correct?"

"You got it!"

"Good, so I email Eye, request a regression session for this Saturday at your apartment if a slot is available, or the next Saturday if this Saturday is booked up?"

"Yes, just remember I am known as Streetwalker."

"Right. I'm glad you reminded me of that."

"When you hear from her, please let me know."

"I will do that. Thank you again for everything."

"You are welcome, again."

9

On Dacque's advice, Connie arrived at his apartment around nine thirty for her ten o'clock appointment with Eyeonthepast. Dani and Dacque were waiting for her.

Dani was almost as excited as Connie about her first, past life regression session. "Are you nervous?" she inquired.

"Of course," Connie replied. "Is that unusual?"

"Heck no. It proves you are normal."

"I guess that is comforting," Connie responded with little conviction in her voice.

Dani laughed out loud. "Dacque will go over the procedure with you for a few minutes while we are waiting. That should help you relax a bit."

"I hope so."

"There is really nothing to be nervous about," Dacque assured her. "Eyeonthepast will get you settled into the easy chair over in the corner where I have placed a dining room chair for her to sit on. She will set up her CD recorder on the end table there. She will put one of her soothing, sounds-of-nature CDs in my player over in the entertainment center. She will give you instructions on how to become more and more relaxed. Keep in mind that she is a pro at this, and she will lead you along into a hypnotic state and start asking you questions. Even though you will be hypnotized, you will be able to remember most of the information that you reveal to her. You will also have the CD recordings to refer to later. Any questions that you can think of?"

"I cannot think of anything."

"Great."

"When you are finished," Dani added, "Eye will likely be in a hurry to run out the door to her next appointment so call me on my cell phone and we will return and answer any questions that you may have. Dacque has informed me that he already advised you concerning what information can and cannot be shared with others, so you need to be cautious about what you say to us."

"I understand."

10

Dacque's front door buzzer sounded at five minutes after ten. "Hello."

"Good morning, it's Eye. I am running a little late."

Dacque buzzed her in and then opened his apartment door so she could walk directly in. Dacque and the ladies waited just inside the door and listened for the sound of the elevator stopping at the third floor. Eye charged through the open apartment door and almost collided with the awaiting threesome. After a hasty introduction, Dacque advised Eye that he already prepped Cancan on the general process and then he and Dani took their leave.

"Any questions before we get started?" Eye asked Cancan.

"I don't think so. Streetwalker gave me a pretty good synopsis of the process."

"Great. Please get yourself comfortably settled in the recliner and I will play us some relaxing tunes compliments of Mother Nature."

Eyeonthepast started the CD and hustled over to the recliner where Cancan sat watching her. "We are not going to hustle through our entire session but the more I motor along through the preliminaries the more time I have left for the main event."

Cancan grinned. "I understand."

"Good. First off, I would like you to close your eyes and try to ignore any noise I may make. I need you to picture a beautiful, relaxing scene. It does not matter if you were ever there, or it came from a movie or even one that you sometimes imagine you would love to travel to. Think of your beautiful scenery, feel the relaxing music and banish all other thoughts from your mind."

Eye proceeded to unpack her CD player and set it up on the end table next to the recliner. She then slightly repositioned the dining room chair left there for her by Streetwalker and settled down on it. "Now I would like you to go through a process where you will start down at your toes and concentrate on relaxing them specifically. Then gradually move this relaxation process one step at a time along your feet, up your legs, then torso until you reach your neck. Then skip down to your fingertips and work your way back up to your neck again but this time continue along through your face to the top of your head. Throughout the entire relaxing process, I would like you to take full, deep breaths."

Eye paused and watched for three or four minutes or so. "You are now in a very, very relaxed state and I will momentarily begin counting from one to ten and when you next hear the word ten you will be hypnotized and respond to my suggestions and questions. One... two... three... you are beginning to feel sleepy, four... five... six... seven you are now feeling very, very sleepy but you will not fall asleep, eight... nine... ten. You are now in a deep hypnotic state."

Eyeonthepast lifted Cancan's left hand off of her lap and raised it up above their heads. She then placed it on top of her own left hand before gradually lowering them downwards and back to Cancan's lap. "I would now like you to travel back in time to when you were twenty and then keep going back to when you were fifteen and continue back to when you were ten. Think of a very happy event that took place when you were ten and tell me about it."

"I went to my first ballet dancing class that year."

"Why did that make you so happy?"

"I had been hounding my mother forever to allow me to take ballet lessons and when she asked me what I wanted for my tenth birthday I told her dancing lessons. She finally said yes."

"Cool! I now would like you to keep going back further in time to when you were younger and younger and tell me about a happy event when you were four."

"It is my fourth birthday and Mommy and Daddy bought me my first Barbie Doll set with lots of clothes I could change her into."

"That is wonderful. I need you to continue travelling back in time to when you were three and then two and still back further to when you were one. Keep on going back to when you were first born and then to before you were born. Picture yourself in a gently sloping, non-confining tunnel like one that might be found in a children's playground. As you slide further and further along you see a light at the end of the tunnel that gradually becomes brighter and brighter as you get closer to the bottom. When you reach the end of the tunnel you will land gently on your feet in one of your previous lifetimes. Let me know when you are out of the tunnel."

"I am out of the tunnel."

"Please tell me what you see or what you are doing."

"We are arriving at the house of our Grand-Mere and Grand-Pere."

"What is your name?"

"Mourning Dove"

"Who is arriving with you?"

"My mother and father and my little sister, Spring Time."

"Where do your Grand-Mere and Grand-Pere live?"
"Ville DuSable."
"Where is Ville DuSable located?"
"On the south shore of the Chicago River."
"What year is it?"
"1812"
"How old are you, Mourning Dove?"
"Ten."
"Why are you visiting with your Grand-Mere and Grand-Pere on this trip?"
"My father is going off to check his trap lines and when he does this we usually go to stay with my grandparents until he returns."
"What is your father's name?"
"Tomtatuk."
"Where do you live?"
"In the village."
"What is the name of the village?"
"It does not have a name. It is our Indian village."
"What is the name of your Indian tribe?"
"The Potawatomi."
"What is your mother's name?"
"Francine."
"Is she French?"
"Yes."
"What is your Grand-Mere's name?"
"Claudette Dupuis."
"And your Grand-Pere's name?"
"Henri Dupuis."
"Is your Grand-Pere also a trapper?"
"No."
"What does he do?"
"He works in the trading post."
"Does he own the trading post?"

"No, he works for Monsieur DuSable."

"How many languages can you speak, Mourning Dove, and what are they?"

"Three. Potawatomi, Francais, and some English I have learned from the English trappers who come to the trading post."

"That sounds like a very interesting lifetime that you have, Mourning Dove. I would now like you to tell me if any of the people you know in 1812 are incarnated with you again in your current lifetime and if so please tell me their names in 1812 and also today."

"My father Tomtatuk is Dacque LaRose and my sister Spring Time is Dani Christian."

Eyeonthepast removed the CD from her player and replaced it with a new one.

"I would like you once again to imagine that you are in the tunnel you were sliding down before and this time when you exit from the tunnel you will be in a past lifetime different from your one as Mourning Dove. Please let me know when you are out of the tunnel."

"I am out of the tunnel."

"Please tell me what you see or what you are doing."

"We are all around my brother's bed. He is very sick."

"Oh, I am very sorry to hear that. What is your name?"

"Zara."

"What is your brother's name?"

"Zianos."

"Is your brother in a hospital or in your home, or somewhere else?"

"In our home."

"How old are you, Zara?"

"Six."

"How old is Zianos?"

"Six."

"Are you twins?"

"Yes."

"Do you know your last name?"

"Amendola."

"Do you know why Zianos is very sick?"

"Mommy calls it TB. It has a very long name that I cannot remember."

"Do you know what year it is?"

"1910."

"Is your house in a town or out in the country?"

"In the country."

"Do you know the name of the town or city where your Mommy and Daddy go to buy food and other things?"

"Anywhere."

Two quick incarnations in a row in the same town. That is a first; I am pretty sure, Eyeonthepast thought to herself. "What is your Mommy's name?"

"Mommy."

"What name does your Daddy call your Mommy?"

"Bettina."

"What name does your Mommy call your Daddy?"

"Italo."

Eye desperately wanted to advance Cancan's memory of her incarnation as Zara onward a couple of years and find out how Zianos made out, but she knew better. If Zara's brother did not win his battle with TB, then she would likely have a sobbing six-year-old on her hands and that she did not need. "Thank you for that information, Zara. I would like you now to look at the people you know there in 1910 and tell me if any of them are incarnated again with you in this lifetime. If they are, please give their names in 1910 and their names today."

"My Daddy then is my husband today, Carson Cantland. My Mommy then is our daughter Camille."

Eyeonthepast inserted a new CD in the player next to her.

"Thank you very much for that information. I would like you one last time to imagine that you are in the same tunnel sliding towards the light at the bottom. When you exit from the tunnel you will land in a past lifetime other than your two past lives as Zara and Mourning Dove. Please let me know when you are out of the tunnel."

"I am out of the tunnel."

"Please tell me what you see or what you are doing."

"We have just landed on the shores of the land of Yuca."

"Who do you mean when you say we?"

"Our leader, Iltar, and our small group of individuals who volunteered to accompany him to the land of Yuca."

"Where did you sail from?"

"The city of Poseidia."

"Where is the city of Poseidia located?"

"On the island of Poseidia."

"Can you give me some sense of where the island of Poseidia is located by describing its location in terms used in modern geography?"

"It was the largest remaining island in the continent of Atlantis before the final, major destruction and was situated about a thousand miles east of Mexico."

"Thank you. That helps. What is the purpose of your trip to the land of Yuca?"

"The Gods have advised some of us Atlanteans that the next major destruction of our once prosperous nation will effectively cause the remaining islands to disappear into the ocean. Our leaders want the records of our history and scientific knowledge to be saved for future generations and detailed copies of these are being sent to selected locations with our migrating citizens, like us. We have for many centuries been able to travel by air and water to visit with various foreign cities around the world and are on friendly terms with most of them, including the Yuca tribe. We hope to receive cooperation and assistance from the Yuca tribe to construct safe vaults in which to store our valuable documents. We have no way of knowing how the surface of remaining continents will be changed during the final destruction of Atlantis, but we hope that some of our records will be saved."

"That is interesting. What is your name?"

"Ishtar."

"Are you a man or a woman?"

"A man."

"Are there any female migrants in your group?"

"Only a few. Part of our mission includes intermarrying with the Yuca maidens to demonstrate the sincerity of our intensions."

"How many men and women are there in your group of migrants?"

"There are twenty men and five wives."

"Do you have any relatives in your group of migrants?"

"My brother, Ishtel."

"I would like you to check over your group of migrants from Poseidia and see if you recognize anyone who you know in your current life, and if there are some please identify them in both lifetimes."

"My brother Ishtel is my father today, Carman Gannon."

"Thank you very much for all of the information that you have shared with me today. I am now going to begin to bring you out of your hypnotic trance state. As I count down from ten to one you will gradually become more and more aware of your current surroundings and when I again say the word one you will remember most of the information you revealed today but you will no longer be hypnotized. Ten... nine... eight, you are beginning to wake up, seven... six... five... four, you are now even more awake, three... two... one. Wake up!"

Cancan rubbed her eyes and looked around the unfamiliar apartment trying to remember where she was.

Eye was over at the entertainment center retrieving her nature CD for her next session. "I wish I could stay and chat with you for a few minutes," she said to Cancan as she packed up her CD player and handed Cancan her three CDs, "but I am on the run to one more session for this morning. You can discuss your Mourning Dove incarnation with Dacque and Dani but the other two should probably remain a secret for now."

"You know their names? I thought we were supposed to keep our names a secret?"

Eye grinned. "Yes, we are, but Dacque and Dani's names have shown up so many times in various sessions that I now know who they are, and it is obvious you also know them, or they would not have been waiting here with you for my arrival."

"That makes sense," Cancan replied. "Thank you very much for taking some of your precious time to hold this session for me. The information we uncovered can only be described as mindboggling."

"You are welcome. Maybe we will meet again," Eye said and headed for the door.

11

As soon as Eyeonthepast was on her way to her next morning session, Connie called Dani's cell phone. She and Dacque were only a block away from Dacque's apartment at the time so they returned within five minutes.

"Well, how did it go?" Dani eagerly asked.

"Unbelievable!" Connie declared with a wide grin.

"I'll take that as unbelievably good and not unbelievably bad?"

"Definitely, unbelievably good."

"Super. What can you tell us?"

"Right off, the first past life I talked about involved you two."

Dacque and Dani smiled at each other. "Good old England?" Dani asked.

"Actually, no," Connie replied with a frown. "It was on the south shore of the Chicago River."

"Tomtatuk?" Dacque asked.

"That's it."

"Who were you?"

"I was your first daughter, Mourning Dove."

"Was your mother Francine?"

"Yes, but I could not identify her."

"That is because you have not met her yet, but you will very, very soon, I promise you that."

"I will?"

"She lives in your subdivision about two blocks away from you."

"You're kidding? How can that be, and I have not yet met her?"

"There is a lot of information you still do not know about souls and their activities because you are pretty new at this. Here is a brief explanation which may help you understand for now. Souls seem to belong to groups, so some soul-group members reincarnate together time and again as they work on actions or Karma from previous lifetimes. Before the next round of incarnations some of the souls in the group determine a basic plan for their next lives together. You, Dani, and I, along with the reincarnated Francine, as well as many others, all planned to be here in Anywhere now, in this incarnation. The reincarnated Francine came from New York State, I came from Ohio, and Dani came here from Dallas, but the group of us being here together was all preplanned."

"You mean our souls preplan our entire lives?"

"Yes and no. Ours souls come up with the ideal plan for our lives, but we also have free will to do as we choose so in most instances our preplanned goals are never entirely achieved."

"Okay, I have the basic gist of it even if I do not understand it entirely," Connie stated.

"You said I was there also?" Dani asked.

"Yes. Have you not uncovered that incarnation?"

"No, but I only received one regression session. Dacque, how much can she tell me?"

"I would say no details other than your relationship to Connie and me."

"Okay," Connie said. "You were my younger sister and Dacque's apparently second daughter."

"Neat! I am glad I discovered that," Dani replied.

"My other two past lives were also quite interesting," Connie continued. "My family apparently experienced our most recent past life with this Zianos spirit that Cammi keeps talking about, and the third one I talked about was way, way back where I was part of a group migrating from Poseidia or Atlantis to apparently Mexico, to try and preserve Atlantis' history and scientific knowledge because the rest of the original Atlantis was on the verge of a final destruction."

"Wow, they both sound quite exciting," Dani declared.

"Do you guys have any other questions before I take off? I know Carson will be eager to find out how it went."

"Is he going to have a regression session too?" Dani asked.

"He was sort of sitting on the fence until I found out how my session went but I suspect he will be pretty keen after I report back to him on what I discovered, in general terms of course. Are you still coming over to our place today to visit with Cammi, Dacque?"

"I can if you like. I already have a new storybook for her."

Connie grinned. "She loved the last one and when I told her you might visit again this afternoon, she was quite pleased."

"I guess that clinches it," Dacque declared.

12

Dacque arrived at the Cantland home around two o'clock, just like the previous Saturday, and after he rang the doorbell the door was opened by Cammi.

"Good afternoon, Cammi. It is nice to see you again."

"Hello Mr. LaRose. Come in, please."

Dacque had deliberately held Cammi's surprise behind his back as he waited for the door to be opened but once he was inside the foyer, he handed the package, wrapped in red paper, to Cammi. Her smile could melt ice cubes and Dacque's heart skipped a beat or two. He could do this every Saturday for the remainder of his life, he thought to himself.

"Thank you, Mr. LaRose. Mommy and Daddy are waiting for us in the living room. Please come with me."

Connie and Carson said hello but did not get up out of their chairs, allowing Cammi to continue her duties as hostess for the day. "May I open the present now, Mommy?"

"Yes, dear. Go right ahead."

Cammi quickly tore the paper off of her gift and held the book out in front of her so she could read the title. "Michael's first heli…cop…ter ride. Thank you, Mr. LaRose."

"You are very welcome, Cammi. Would you like me to read it to you again today?"

"Yes, please, Mr. LaRose."

Dacque settled down at the end of the sofa and Cammi quickly snuggled up beside him. His heart did a couple more leapfrogs as he felt her warm body against his arm and he quickly started to read Cammi her new storybook. At the conclusion of the story Cammi headed off to her room to place her gift on the bookshelf and play with her toys.

"That went much better than last week," Dacque declared.

Connie laughed. "She has you pegged as the next best thing to Santa Claus."

"I won't complain," Dacque responded with a laugh.

"Cammi is probably out of range by now, and I want to tell you more about our lifetime with Zianos. I broke Eye's rules and filled Carson in on the details even though he has not received a regression session. I guess I am going to break them again by telling you what I revealed under hypnosis about that recent incarnation, but because I did not identify you as being part of our lives there then I assume you were not involved with us in that incarnation."

"That is probably correct."

"In 1910, Zianos was very ill with tuberculosis. I was his twin sister, Zara. We were six years old. Carson was our father. His name then was Italo Amendola. Our mother was Cammi. Her name was Bettina. If that isn't shocking enough, we lived out in the country near Anywhere."

"Wow. I don't think I have ever heard of two quick incarnations in the same city before."

"Eye said that as well. She never asked how Zianos made out, but I suspect he did not survive his illness."

"Keep in mind that she was dealing with you as a six-year-old and was probably worried that you could get hysterical talking about losing your twin brother. She was not prepared to take that risk."

"That is what I figured, too. After uncovering these past lifetimes together for our entire family, it makes Cammi's story about her friend Zianos totally believable. Do you still think that Zianos is an earthbound spirit or could his soul be hanging around to be with the rest of us?"

"Good question. I think it could be either, to be perfectly honest."

"What do you think we should do now?"

"With this new information, I think it is you, as his twin sister, who is in a better position than me, a total stranger to that lifetime, to try and make contact with Zianos."

"I don't know anything about talking to spirits. You have the experience, not me."

"I know, but I am certain he is more likely to communicate with you than me. I will advise you along the way, okay?"

"I guess so. Why would he make contact with Cammi instead of me in the first place?"

"I think it is the age similarity with her. When he was alive with you, he was very attached to both of you as his twin sister and mother. It doesn't get any closer than that. It is also an established fact that young children like Cammi, who were quite recently in spirit form themselves, are more likely to see spirits than adults, even though they do not understand the difference between spirit friends and human friends."

"So, what am I supposed to do now?"

"Well, for starters, whenever Cammi is not around, I would suggest you go into her room and try to talk to Zianos. He probably hangs around there a lot. Share with him the information you now have about your relationship with him in the past and tell him you want to see him and talk to him again like you did as twins. I believe that he will find this information very appealing."

"That makes sense. It is not often that I am home without Cammi, but it does happen."

"It is possible that we can locate the birth and death records for your earlier family, if you are interested in that?"

"Is there any real value in it?"

"I am not really sure. At least you would know whether Zianos survived his bout of tuberculosis or died young. That might come in handy in your conversing with him."

"Okay. I am pretty busy with a full-time job and a home to keep. Any chance you would volunteer to look into the old records for me?"

Dacque smiled. "Yes, I will check into it for you. I was not going to do it if you did not want the answers, but if you write down all of the information you received from the regression session then I will see what I can find."

"Great, thank you." Connie went to retrieve a pen and notepad.

13

Lois Maria Santini, usually called Mary, was abandoned by her father at age seven. At age fifteen, the police and Child Care Services swooped into her mother's apartment one evening and trotted Mary off to Foster Care, supposedly because her mother had been arrested for some reason, but this was never confirmed to Mary. Her first foster care placement was terminated abruptly when she complained to her foster care supervisor that the man of the house was harassing her with offers to teach her about sex. Her second foster care placement was terminated abruptly when the nice family's teenage son would not stop hounding her about climbing into bed with him.

With no other suitable home placements available to her Mary was sent to a Temp House, which was in effect a bunk house for children under the care of the Foster Care agency who could not be placed in an appropriate home at the time. She soon became buddies with a boy in the Temp House who was in some of her High School classes. They were the two oldest residents in the Temp House at the time. Wandering the streets one Saturday morning, the two buddies came across an almost packed moving van. They peeked inside the moving van out of curiosity and her buddy shocked her when he suggested they climb inside and see where they ended up. After what she had gone through over the past few months, Mary welcomed the opportunity to escape from her miserable life in her hometown. Six or seven hours later they were homeless street people in a city they did not even know the name of.

Mary's buddy, Al, had previously been advised by an older childcare ward that the secret to survival on the streets was to quickly locate the soup kitchens and the missions for the homeless, and that is precisely what they did. As the weather showed signs of approaching winter, Mary and Al hopped an empty train car travelling south. This brought them into warmer surroundings, but winter kept following them, so they soon hitchhiked further south, beginning a routine they followed to stay ahead of the bad weather. Mary and Al did not spend all of their time together and often spent their days in different activities and locations, but always agreed on which mission they would meet up at in the evening. When Al did not show up at their designated location three nights in a row, Mary knew something was wrong. She did not want to accept the possibility that she had been abandoned once more, so she assumed that Al had been arrested for something and she decided it was time for her to move on to another city once again.

Mary reluctantly hitchhiked out of town the next morning, alone, fully aware of the risk she was assuming as a girl hitchhiking by herself, but not caring very much because of the miserable life she had lived for sixteen years. Fortunately, she was picked up by a compassionate business lady who was travelling to the city of Anywhere for an appointment and was happy to have some company on the two-hour drive. She dropped Mary off in front of Anywhere's Downtown Mission and Mary had a new home in the sunny south.

INVISIBLE FRIENDS

Mary liked her new city and settled into her new routine. She made some acquaintances but no good friends like Al. One evening on her walk back to the Downtown Mission, a severe thunderstorm was rumbling overhead, and she knew she was not going to make it back to the mission before getting drenched. Passing by the 7th Street Apartment Complex she decided to check the parking lot to see if anyone had accidently left a car door unlocked and got lucky. She found an unlocked rear door just as the drizzling rain was beginning so she hopped in, at least until the rain stopped. It did not stop so Mary eventually fell asleep on the dry, rear seat.

Dacque LaRose lived in one of the buildings in the 7th Street Apartment Complex. He always checked to make sure he locked all of his doors when he parked his car because he did not have an automatic door locking system in his older model vehicle. The night before Mary encountered her unwelcome thunderstorm, Dacque had been awakened around five in the morning after a vivid dream. Dreams were one of the ways that the Heavenly Powers sent him messages. This message was simple. He was instructed to leave a car door open that evening as someone needed his protection. No other details, but Dacque new his messages from the Heavenly Powers were both real and reliable, so he faithfully left the rear door on the driver's side open on his car that evening.

Once again, around five in the morning, Dacque received a new dream and a more detailed message that there was a teenage girl sleeping in the back seat of his car. He was told in his dream that she used the name Mary Smith, but it was not her real name, that she often told people she was eighteen, but she was not, and to go out and get her and keep her safe. Dacque reluctantly but obediently got dressed, grabbed a flashlight, and traipsed out to his car. He woke up the sleeping squatter in the back seat and as she started to escape through the other door, he shouted out her alias, *Mary Smith! Don't run away!* She turned towards Dacque to check if he was someone she knew from the soup kitchens and he proceeded to tell her that he knew she told people she was eighteen, but she was not and that he was instructed to protect her.

Mary had the other door unlocked and her hand on the door handle, but she noted that Dacque was making no effort to grab or attack her and was only talking to her. She asked how he knew this information about her, and he told her he received messages in dreams from the Heavenly Powers. She found that hard to believe but decided to listen to his continuing explanations as she knew she could escape in one second and easily outrun this old man if necessary.

It took a lot of persuading but eventually Dacque was able to convince Mary to let him prove his story to her because each time he received messages from the Heavenly Powers he wrote them down on the pad he always kept on the night table beside his bed. He could show the notes on his pad to her if she would go inside with him. The suggestion that she go up to his bedroom with him immediately set off new alarm bells in Mary's head and she accused him of just being some dirty old man. This did not alarm Dacque because he half expected it, but he was prepared with a counter suggestion. He proposed that Mary keep a safe distance away from him as they entered his apartment building and once outside his apartment door, he would fetch his longest butcher knife from a kitchen drawer and give it to her for her protection.

That proposal caught Mary's attention and she asked why he was not concerned that she might use it to threaten him and rob him. His explanation sealed the deal. He explained that God or the Heavenly Powers occasionally asked him to help people like her in need, and that the Heavenly Powers would not send him to help someone who would turn around and harm him. Mary had to admit to herself that his reasoning made sense, so she took a chance on trusting this stranger who had not made any move to harm her.

Mary and her trusty butcher knife moved into Dacque's guest room, with a locked door, and she and Dacque soon developed a trusting, granddaughter-grandfather relationship. After meeting Dani Christian and listening to her recount how Dacque had been guided to help her by the Heavenly Powers in a time of need, Mary revealed to Dacque that she sometimes experienced a recurring dream where she was running away from something or someone she did not see in the dream. She was wearing old-fashioned shoes and a long dress that she would never wear now, but somehow felt that the girl or woman in the dream was really her. Dacque suspected that this recurring dream of Mary's was actually a glimpse from one of her past lives and when he mentioned this to Mary, he was shocked that she agreed with him. He was also shocked at how much knowledge she had picked up about reincarnation from movies, television shows and by reading books.

Over a number of weeks Mary's interest in reincarnation and the Reincarnation Enlightenment Group increased and culminated in her receiving her first hypnotic regression session. She discovered that her recurring dreams were in fact actual scenes from an interesting past lifetime which included being Francine, the squaw of Tomtatuk, an earlier incarnation of Dacque's in Ville DuSable.

14

Heath, Rosalie, and their youngest daughter, Raluca Westgate, their only offspring still living at home, are friends of Dacque's and reincarnation researchers as well. Raluca is one year older than Mary and the two of them have become close friends. Once Raluca got to know Mary better she realized that Mary was blessed with above average intelligence. Raluca was disturbed by the fact that Mary only had a grade ten education and seemed to have no opportunity to continue her education as a runaway from the Foster Care system in a northern state.

Mary was determined to conceal her true identity until she turned eighteen, because she did not want to be found by whatever authorities might be looking for a Mary or Maria Santini, and that was when she assumed the alias Mary Smith. Unfortunately, Mary Smith could not register at any school because she had no past. When Mary experienced her first regression session with Eyeonthepast she not only discovered her past life in Ville DuSable with Dacque, but a much earlier past lifetime in Bouillon back in 1087 when it was a thriving French community in what is today Belgium. In her regression session Mary identified her mother in Bouillon as being reincarnated now as Rosalie Westgate and her sister Cecile in Bouillon as Raluca Westgate.

When Raluca discovered that Mary had been her sister Angelique in Bouillon she became even more determined to help Mary get back into school and obtain an education that would improve her lot in life way beyond what Mary had been cursed with for her first sixteen years. She devised a longshot but ingenious plan to try and allow Mary to continue her education in the rapidly approaching new school year. She first needed to convince her mother and father to offer to become Mary's foster parents in the city of Anywhere. Heath was the only income earner in the household at that time, but he was the owner of his own heating and cooling business, and they were far from destitute. It also did not hurt that Heath received a past life regression session as well and discovered that he too had been in the Bouillon community back in 1087 but part of a different family than Rosalie, Raluca, and Mary.

Heath, as well as Rosalie and Raluca, was well versed in the popular theory of reincarnationists that our souls plan a basic course for our lives before the group of souls reincarnate again, and with Mary's discovered past life connections to their household it was more than just plain simple luck that Mary ended up in the city of Anywhere, out of all of the locations she could have migrated to as she bounced from city to town on her journey south. It did not take that much pleading by Raluca and Rosalie to get Heath to agree to pursue step two of Raluca's ingenious plan.

Convincing Dad was easy compared to achieving step two, and Raluca knew that was where the longshot was going to be, yet she firmly believed that Mary's soul was predestined to join their family so longshot or not it was going to be achieved, somehow. Raluca needed a good solicitor to negotiate with the government authorities in charge of Child Care in the city of

Anywhere, and also in the jurisdiction up north that Mary ran away from a year earlier. Heath never spared the praise he lavished on his solicitor and friend, Nathan Brockinhire, so Raluca asked her father to ask Mr. Brockinhire to represent them in this endeavor, or if he did not feel qualified in this particular area of legal negotiations then to connect them with a solicitor who was more suited to this challenge.

Heath called his friend on the Sunday afternoon when Raluca sprung her plan on him. Nathan was intrigued enough when Heath outlined Raluca's objective and scheme that he joined them in their living room within fifteen minutes to listen to the details. The legal problem with Foster Care is that the local town, city, county, or whatever name the jurisdiction uses, generally has a responsibility to finance the expenses of foster care children. This meant the city of Anywhere would not be eager to inherit dependent runaways from other jurisdictions, so they generally shipped back home runaways from these other jurisdictions. On the other hand, from a financial point of view, the jurisdiction where the runaway ran away from is quite happy to have the expense of providing for that foster child removed from their books. Everyone knew that the main hurdle they needed to leap over successfully was the Foster Care authorities in the city of Anywhere. Nathan Brockinhire was a good choice for this project as he knew the movers and shakers in Anywhere.

Nathan needed to interview Mary because at that point in time no one knew her real name or the city that she had deserted when she hopped into the back of the moving van for a Saturday adventure which turned out to be much more than she ever anticipated. Dacque drove Mary over to the Westgate's home as soon as he received their telephone call. Nathan Brockinhire and Mary journeyed down to Heath's home-office in their basement for privacy. Mary liked Raluca's plan as long as it did not cause her to be shipped back to her original home city, so she would only reveal her personal information to Nathan if he agreed not to reveal it to the wrong people, and he agreed.

As everyone anticipated, the stumbling block turned out to be the Anywhere Foster Care authorities because they had no desire to assume the financial responsibility for the out-of-state runaway, but they sympathetically agreed to be co-operative in every other aspect of the plan presented by Nathan Brockinhire, except financial responsibility. They would oversee Mary's safety and counselling like any other foster care child under their care and would make the arrangements with Mary's home jurisdiction to transfer her legal responsibility to them, but the Westgates would not receive any financial support from the city of Anywhere.

The ball was back in the Westgate's court. Heath had to assume all of Mary's expenses. Raluca, as Daddy's baby girl, knew how to charm her father so it was not too difficult to convince Heath to agree to be financially responsible for Mary, while she was living in their house with them, until she was able to complete high school. At that time, the arrangement would be reexamined to see if it would be continued. And that is how Mary Santini came to be living in the subdivision two blocks away from the home of Carson, Connie, and Cammi Cantland.

15

With Mary in school and Connie at work every weekday Dacque deduced that the bringing together of these two lovely young ladies, from his previous incarnation as Tomtatuk along the banks of the Chicago River in Ville DuSable, as well as in this life, would need to occur on a weekend. The ladies agreed that ten o'clock on the coming Saturday morning, exactly one week almost to the minute following Connie's first regression session, would be the ideal time. Dacque did not argue and gladly sacrificed his standard morning walk in favor of this eagerly anticipated gathering at his apartment.

Past life reunions were not new to Mary or Dacque. Mary participated in a Bouillon reunion a couple of months previously at the Westgates' home when Raluca, Rosalie, Heath, and Mary listened to each other's CDs from their lives together back in the 1080s.

Dacque drove over to the Westgate residence for nine in the morning to say hello and pick up Mary early so they could spend some quality time together, before Connie's anticipated arrival for the Ville DuSable reunion. Dacque and Mary found little time to get together since the school year started. It was quite an adjustment for him to see her only occasionally after having her around pretty much twenty-four seven when she resided in his spare room, before making the big move to secure her future by going back to school as a foster care ward of the Westgates. Connie arrived at five minutes to ten and Dacque introduced her to Mary but deliberately refrained from mentioning to either of them any specific details of their past life connections.

Dacque explained to Connie that they would listen to their three CDs from their Ville DuSable incarnations in the chronological order that these incarnations were discovered, and after each one they could discuss anything that anyone wished to discuss before they moved on to the next CD. Dacque inserted his CD in the player and pressed the start button.

The scene that Dacque landed in when he slid out the end of Eyeonthepast's imaginary tunnel was his wedding ceremony in the little chapel in Ville DuSable, presided over by Father Jacques. Tomtatuk was a purebred Potawatomi and the marriage ceremony was conducted in French, so he did not understand much of what was taking place. Tomtatuk had decided that he would like Francine to be his squaw and he worked on courting her, Indian style, for over a year as he patiently taught her to speak some Potawatomi and she taught him some French. Over time she realized her attraction to this mighty specimen of a kind, gentle native was undeniable, and she agreed to be his squaw.

Francine's parents, Claudette and Henri Dupuis, grew to appreciate Tomtatuk's qualities the more he continued to visit with Francine, and they finally acceded to her pleadings with one condition; they would have to be married in the village chapel. The ceremony was attended by Tomtatuk's brother, Strong Eagle, Francine's parents, Henri's employer Monsieur DuSable and his wife, and a few close friends from the settlement. The only individual that Dacque was able to identify was that Tomtatuk's brother Strong Eagle was reincarnated with him again as his son, Richard LaRose. When he received this reading, he had never met Connie or Mary.

Dacque had deliberately not watched the reactions of the ladies as they listened to him describe this scene from his Ville DuSable past life until the recording concluded. Both ladies were wiping tears from their cheeks and Mary suddenly jumped off of the sofa and charged over towards Dacque who quickly hopped out of his recliner in the corner just fast enough for her to fly into his open arms. Mary sobbed on his shoulder for two or three minutes before she relinquished her vice-like hold on Dacque's back.

"Have you got some tissues, please?" Mary asked in a breaking voice.

Dacque's eyes were also red but Mary probably did not even notice. He hustled out to the kitchen and returned with the box of tissues. After she removed a handful, Dacque walked the box over to Connie.

"That was a tearjerker, I must admit," Connie said as she pulled out a couple of tissues.

Mary and Dacque never listened to each other's CDs from Ville DuSable following Mary's regression session because in it, Mary effectively revealed her true identity by identifying the names of her parents. She told Dacque at the time that she did not wish to place him in a position where he might someday need to choose between his loyalty to her and possibly lying to the police, or childcare service workers on knowing her true identity. In good time, she assured him, they would share the information on their CDs.

After the threesome recovered their composures, Dacque asked the ladies if they had any questions. Receiving none, Dacque accepted Mary's CD and placed it in his player.

The scene from their past lives together described by the in-trance Mary was how Francine first met Tomtatuk. She was out in the woods that surrounded Ville DuSable, picking berries for dinner, when this native on a pony came charging through the trees towards her. Her first reaction was to run, which she did. This scene of her running through the woods looking over her shoulder had been a scene she experienced over a period of a few years in a number of dreams. She saw this woman in a long dress and old-fashioned shoes running as best she could and every few seconds glancing over her shoulder. In the dream she never saw what or who she was running from.

Eye coaxed some details out of Mary concerning what followed next. Apparently, the native on the pony did not see her until she started running, and when he did, he slowed down and just allowed his pony to walk along a fair distance behind her. The frightened woman did not stop or slow down but continued to run and suddenly performed a flying belly flop over a tree root. The native hopped off of his horse and walked or ran to where she was sprawled. He then stood over her with his hand out saying "Up. Up."

She reached up and gave him her hand, and he pulled her to a standing position. He stood there and watched as she brushed the leaves and dirt off of her dress and then said, "Up, horse. Tomtatuk take trading post." She walked over to the Indian pony and Tomtatuk lifted her up on the saddleless horse. She straddled the animal as ladylike as possible in her long dress and held on to the mane of the pony as Tomtatuk walked it to the trading post. She thanked him and ran off home, without any berries for dinner.

Eyeonthepast asked if she saw much of him after that and she said yes, he started hanging around more and more as time passed and after she turned eighteen, he asked if she would be his squaw. She accepted his offer.

Eye asked Mary what her name was in this incarnation, amongst other things, and she indicated she was Francine

Dupuis and age fifteen in 1798. She identified Tomtatuk as Dacque, her parents Claudette and Henri Dupuis as her parents again, Laura and Luigi Santini.

This time, as the recording stopped, it was Connie that was doing the sobbing. "It is totally amazing how we came up with the same basic information," she said between sobs, "on three different occasions and during three different described scenes. Anyone who claims this is not real is simply spouting off, showing their total ignorance."

Dacque and Mary nodded their agreement and allowed Connie to regain her composure and dry off her cheeks. "It is nice to hear how Tomtatuk and Francine first met and how we progressed towards our actual marriage ceremony," Dacque said to Mary while they waited for Connie.

Dacque placed Connie's CD in the player and started it spinning. The threesome listened as Connie described the family's arrival at her grandparent's home in Ville DuSable for a short stay while Tomtatuk went off to check his trap lines. Connie identified Tomtatuk as Dacque and her sister Spring Time as Dani Christian. She identified her mother as Francine but could not connect her to Mary as she only met Mary for the first time less than an hour earlier.

There were no tears this time when the CD turned silent. "How come Dani is not here with us?" Mary asked.

"She has not yet discovered her incarnation as Spring Time so she could not participate in our Ville DuSable reunion today," Dacque responded. "When she does, we will hold another reunion with the four of us. Dani will make sure of that, trust me. She was happy to hear that she was part of this incarnation with us, but she understands why she cannot listen to our CDs until she knows the details of her connection to us. Any other questions?"

"Does Mary know about Cammi and her visitor?" Connie asked.

"She knows I have been visiting with Cammi and reading her stories but that is all."

"How much can I tell her?" Connie asked.

"No names, but I think it will be alright if you reveal your suspicions."

Connie turned to Mary, sitting on the other end of the sofa. "My six-year-old daughter apparently has been receiving visits from a child spirit visitor."

"Neat!" Mary declared. "Is she frightened?"

"She does not seem to be. She just views him as another playmate. I am curious why she has not asked how he just appears at times without entering through the front door like our other visitors, but for now she seems happy to have him visit when he comes. Speaking of Cammi, Dacque told me that you only live two blocks from our house. Are you interested in doing some babysitting for us now and then? Our previous babysitter has gone off to college."

"Sure. I do have some experience helping with younger children."

"Great. Can I have your phone number?" Connie grabbed her purse from the end table beside her and wrote down Mary's telephone number. "Are you still visiting with Cammi this afternoon?" she asked, turning her attention back to Dacque sprawled comfortably in his easy chair in the corner.

Dacque smiled. "Will she be disappointed if I do not show up?"

"Definitely, but let's face it, it will not be possible for you to visit her every Saturday afternoon for eternity so the day will come when your routine will be interrupted. If I tell her ahead of time that you are not coming on a particular day, she will be fine."

"I'll be there around two, as usual, but I just thought of something else we might consider. What do you two ladies think about me bringing Mary with me to your house? It will give Cammi a chance to get acquainted with Mary before she shows up one day to babysit."

"I think that is a wonderful idea," Connie replied. "Are you free to come, Mary? Cammi is a bit shy with newcomers at first so this will be a good opportunity for her to meet you without Mon and Dad being ready to beat it out the front door on her."

"Sounds like a plan," Mary declared.

16

Dacque rang the doorbell at the Cantland residence a little after two on Saturday afternoon. Just like the week before, Cammi opened the door for him but this time Connie and Carson stood behind her.

"Good afternoon, Cammi. I brought a friend today. Her name is Mary."

"Please come in, Mr. LaRose, and Mary."

Dacque followed Mary into the foyer and closed the door behind him. He handed his hostess today's present, this time wrapped in yellow paper.

"Thank you, Mr. LaRose."

"You are very welcome. I am truly enjoying reading the stories to you on my visits. Are you enjoying them too?"

"Oh yes, very much."

"That is good news."

Dacque greeted Connie and Carson, and Connie introduced Mary to her husband before they moved into the living room. Dacque had prepped Mary on their drive over there that he and Cammi settled down on the far end of the sofa and her parents seemed to favor the two living room chairs. When Connie invited Mary to pick any seat she immediately walked over to the near end of the sofa.

"Can I unwrap it now, Mommy?"

"Yes, Dear. Mr. LaRose brings the books for you."

Cammi quickly unwrapped her parcel and looked at the cover. "Tommy Goes to the State Fair." She handed the book to Dacque and climbed up on the sofa next to him.

At approximately halfway through the book Dacque stopped reading. "Mary has lots of experience reading stories to girls your age, Cammi. How about we give her a turn to read to you?"

Cammi looked over at Mary with apparent uncertainty.

"Mr. LaRose is right. I love to read stories to boys and girls like you. How about it?" Mary asked with a smile.

"I guess that is okay," Cammi replied.

Mary read the remainder of the story, stopping a couple of times to point out to Cammi specific items in one of the pictures. "Did you like that story?" she asked Cammi.

"Yes. I think it would be fun to go to the State Fair."

"I think it would be too," Mary responded.

"Did you ever go to the State Fair?"

"No. I lived way up north where they have lots of snow in the winter. The State Fair occurred in the summer, but we lived a long, long way from the place where the State Fair was held so I never did get to visit it."

"That is too bad," Cammi commented sadly.

"Do you like stories?" Mary asked.

"Yes."

"I would love to read you some more stories while I am here if you would like me to?"

Cammi looked at Connie.

"Why don't you take Mary into your room and she can read some of the storybooks in your bookcase, okay?"

"Okay." Cammi hopped off of the sofa and Mary followed along behind her.

After Dacque was sure Cammi and Mary were out of hearing range, he sprung with the news he had been patiently waiting to share with Connie and Carson. "I did some research in the local births and deaths records. Unfortunately, the news is not exactly good, but you probably suspected it would not be. I could not find any birth records for your Amendola family, so it is possible they moved into the Anywhere vicinity from elsewhere and maybe even from another country.

"I did find the death records for Zianos and it appears he likely did not survive his battle with tuberculous. He passed away on October 10th, 1910 and is buried in an old, abandoned, church cemetery, on a back concession road just a few miles out of town. There was a country church there over a century ago called the Oldfield Catholic Church-on-the-Hill. The custom then was to bury the local church members in the graveyard behind the church. The church burnt down and apparently was never rebuilt. Today, the old graveyard is situated in a cattle pasture with a fence around it. I managed to locate the farm owner and received permission to visit the unkept graveyard. It is possible to read some of the names on the few, still-standing tombstones but I could not locate one with Zianos' name on it."

"Thank you for your conscientious research, Dacque," Connie said. "I admit that I was braced for the probable bad news concerning Zianos' illness. I have not had any opportunities to sit in Cammi's room alone and see if Zianos will visit with me, but I will try to do it whenever the opportunity does present itself."

"I understand," Dacque assured her.

"I think it is about time I scheduled a regression session," Carson stated when silence filled the room.

"That is wonderful," Dacque replied. "Would you like to use my apartment as well?"

"I would, thank you, if you do not mind?"

"Great. That's settled. Are you looking at a week today?"

"Yes, if Eyeonthepast has an opening. I will email in my request this afternoon."

"Super."

"I will also request two weeks away if she is filled up this Saturday. Will that work for you?"

"I can make most times work so just let me know when you get the news on your day and time."

"I will do that, thank you again."

Mary read four more stories to Cammi in her room and then deduced that was enough for one visit. Cammi did not suggest that they play any games, so Mary excused herself and returned to the living room.

"How did it go?" Connie asked.

"Fine. We got along great."

"That's what I like to hear. "You have got yourself a part-time job."

Mary grinned. "Sounds good."

Dacque drove Mary the two blocks to her home after an enjoyable day spent with his former apartment guest.

17

Carson Cantland arrived, at Dacque's suggestion, by eight thirty for his nine o'clock appointment with Eyeonthepast on Saturday morning at Dacque's apartment. Dacque briefed him on the general procedure that Eye would follow in preparing him for his first past life regression session. Eyeonthepast arrived at ten minutes before nine and was delighted to find Cantdoit stretched out on Dacque's comfortable lounge chair, ready to get started. Dacque quickly introduced them and as Cantdoit commenced to climb out of the lounger Eye waved him back down and said they would shake hands when she settled in on the chair by his left knee. Dacque quickly departed to meet up with Dani Christian for their prearranged morning walk along 7th street, until Carson called Dani's cell phone to let them know the session was completed.

Eyeonthepast walked over to Dacque's entertainment center and started up her Sounds of Mother Nature CD. She hustled over to Cantdoit, watching her from Dacque's lounge chair, and they shook hands. "I need you to close your eyes now, take full, deep breaths, and try and relax your entire body. Picture a beautiful and soothing scene, real or imagined, while I finish getting ready for our session. Try and ignore any noise I may make and concentrate on the music and your beautiful scenery."

Eye removed her CD player from her carry case and placed it on the end table beside Cantdoit. She set three CD's beside the player and slightly repositioned the chair placed there by Dacque as he always did. With her preparation procedures completed, Eye watched Cantdoit take his deep breaths for two more minutes. "Do not open your eyes. I need you now to concentrate your attention on relaxing one part of your body at a time, starting down at your toes and gradually working your way across your instep then up your legs, and keep on going up your torso to your neck. At that point jump down to your fingertips and work your way up your arms, back to your neck but this time keep moving through your face to the top of your head. Continue taking your deep breaths throughout the entire process."

Eye waited and watched Cantdoit until he appeared to be so relaxed he might fall asleep on her. "I will now begin to count slowly from one to ten and when you next hear the word ten you will enter into a deep hypnotic trance state. One... two... three, you are feeling sleepy, four... five... six... seven, you are feeling very sleepy now, but you will not fall asleep, eight... nine... ten. You are now in a deep hypnotic state. You will follow my instructions and answer the questions that I ask you. Do you understand?"

"Yes."

Eyeonthepast picked up Cantdoit's left hand and slowly raised it upwards until it was over his head before placing it on her own left hand. She then proceeded to slowly lower her hand and watched Cantdoit's hand come down with hers, as if they were one. She inserted a CD in the player and pushed the button. "Picture yourself sliding along in a non-confining, gently sloping tunnel. As you glide along you see a light at the end of the tunnel and it continues to get brighter and brighter as you approach the bottom. When you exit from the tunnel you will land in a past lifetime that is significant to you and your current lifetime. Please let me know when you are out of the tunnel."

"I am out of the tunnel."

"Please describe for me what you see or what you are doing."

"I am pacing the floor in our living room waiting for the midwife and her helper to assist my wife to deliver our first child."

"Are they in the living room with you or in your bedroom?"

"In the bedroom."

"Move along in time until you hear the baby cry and let me know."

"The baby is crying, now. Thank, God."

"Congratulations, Dad."

"Thank you."

"Move along in time to when the midwife brings you your new baby or invites you into the bedroom to visit."

"The door is opening. Oh, my Lord. The midwife is carrying a baby and so is the helper. You have a healthy son and also a healthy daughter, Mr. Amendola., the midwife tells me."

"That is marvelous. Did you and your wife already pick names?"

"Yes. If it was a boy, we planned to call him Zianos and if it was a girl, she would be named Zara."

Those names sound familiar, Eyeonthepast thought to herself. "Those are beautiful names. What is your name, Mr. Amendola?"

"Italo."

"And the name of your wife?"

"Bettina."

"What year is it?"

"1904."

"If any of those present in your house on this occasion are incarnated with you again in your current lifetime, I would like you to tell me their names now and describe your relationship today."

"Bettina is our daughter, Cammi, and Zara is my wife, Connie."

"Thank you very much, Italo, for sharing that information with me. I would like you to once again picture yourself sliding down the same tunnel as before but this time when you exit at the bottom you will land in a different lifetime than your one as Italo. Please let me know when you are out of the tunnel." Eye quickly put a new CD in her player and started it recording.

"I am out of the tunnel."

"Please tell me what you see or what you are doing."

"We are negotiating with some of the settlers from Jamestown."

"Who do you mean when you say we?"

"Chief Powhatan, Opitchapam, Opechancanough and some of the other tribal leaders."

"Do you know the names of the settlers that you are negotiating with?"

"On this occasion there is a William, a John and a James, along with others, but I am never able to remember the strange white man's names."

Eyeonthepast smiled to herself. Interesting to hear the comment from the other side of the fence, she thought to herself. "Are you in Jamestown?"

"No, our village."

"Does it have a name?"

"Werowocomoco."

"Are you negotiating a peace treaty?"

"No. They need some of our food to get them through the winter."

"I see. What year is it?"

"The white men call it 1617."

"Are you at peace with the white men?"

"Most of the time, now. There is always an altercation here and there between some of our tribes and the white men."

"There is more than one tribe? Can you explain, please?"

"Chief Powhatan is the supreme chief over all of our more than thirty tribes."

"What is your name?"

"Potocachan."

"Are you a chief?"

"No. A tribal elder."

"What kind of provisions are the white men asking for?"

"Mainly our corn but they also need some venison and fish supplies."

"What do the white men bring you in trade?"

"Things they bring across the waters in their big ships. Clothing, material of pretty colors for our squaws to make things with, and jewelry we have never seen before."

"That is very interesting, Potocachan. I would like you to look around at the people in the negotiating parties and if you recognize anyone who is incarnated with you in your current lifetime here in Anywhere please identify them in both lifetimes and their relationship to you."

"Opitchapam is my brother Campbell Cantland."

"Thank you for that information. I would now like you to picture yourself back in the tunnel, sliding along slowly towards the light at the bottom, and when you exit from the tunnel this time it will be into a past lifetime other than your lives as Italo or Potocachan. Please let me know when you are out of the tunnel." Eye quickly put a new CD into the player beside her.

"I am out of the tunnel."

"Please tell me what you see or what you are doing."

"Everyone in the palace is in mourning."

"Please explain what has taken place at the palace."

"Our beloved Emperor Charlemagne died yesterday, after being ill for a week."

"Where is the palace located?"

"Aachen."

"Where is Aachen located?"

"The Holy Roman Empire."

"Can you give me some geographical description so I can understand its location?"

"It is north of the Ardennes forest and mountains."

That doesn't help, Eyeonthepast thought to herself. Enough. He can check it out for himself in an atlas. This actually sounds a bit familiar as if I have heard it recently. "What is your name?"

"Edouard Pronovost."

"How old are you?"

"Fifty-one."

"Do you have a wife and family?"

"No."

"Where do you live?"

"At the palace."

"Are you a relative of Charlemagne?"

"No."

"You work at the palace?"

"Yes."

"What is your job at the palace?"

"Primarily I am a guard, but I have other duties at times such as personal attendant and servant."

"Do you enjoy your employment at the palace?"

"Oh yes. Who would not enjoy living in a palace?"

Eye smiled. Good point! "I understand. Will you lose your job at the palace now that Charlemagne has passed away?"

"I don't think so. Charlemagne's son, King Louis, is the new Emperor and he enjoys the time he spends here just as much as his father did."

"Please tell me what year it is?"

"814."

"Please think of the people who are or have been close to you in Aachen and tell me if you recognize any of them in your current lifetime, and if you do, please identify them in both lifetimes."

"My good friend and fellow guard, Jean-Louis Chartrand, is Mary Santini, our new babysitter."

"Thank you, Edouard, for sharing that information with me." Eye stopped the CD player. "I am now going to begin to bring you out of your hypnotic trance. When you awaken you will feel refreshed and remember most of the information that you have shared with me today. On the count of ten, you will awaken. One... two... three, you are starting to become aware of your surroundings, four... five ... six, you are much more aware of your surroundings, seven... eight... nine... ten. Wake up!"

Cantdoit opened his eyes and looked around somewhat bewildered until he recognized Dacque's apartment. Eye returned from Dacque's entertainment center with her Sounds of Mother Nature CD and packed up her CD equipment.

"Here are the CDs from the three incarnations you discovered today," she said, handing them to Cantdoit. "You uncovered some interesting information. Do you remember a lot of what you told me?"

Cantdoit shook his head up and down. "Yes, I think so."

"Good. You are aware of our suggested rules on confidentiality, but you can discuss the incarnations you shared with the people you identified in this lifetime if they have also learned about that particular incarnation. I have to run off to my next session and cannot sit and chat with you."

"I will. Thank you very much, Eye, for doing this for me, and on short notice, too. It was very important to me."

"My pleasure," Eye replied, and hurried towards the door.

18

Dacque and Dani terminated their morning walk as soon as Dani received the phone call from Carson advising her that Eye had departed for her next morning session. Dacque and Dani were back in Dacque's apartment within ten minutes.

"How did it go?" Dani asked as soon as the apartment door was closed.

"Very interesting. I had no inkling that the information I revealed this morning was tucked away in my memory, somehow. I uncovered three totally different past lives. Neither of you were identified in any of them. I will tell you a little bit about each without revealing too much but my logic says that if I did not identify you as being present then we did not share that life together so it should not matter how much I tell you anyway."

"That may sound logical at first glance," Dacque said, "but in a regression session we usually reveal events that occurred over a short period of time, and sometimes people we know can show up unexpectedly twenty or thirty years later in that lifetime, if we decide to investigate time periods down the road, or they do."

"I see what you mean. I did talk about quite-short time periods in my three incarnations. Okay, in the first past life, it did not surprise me when I talked about the spirit we think is visiting with Cammi in her bedroom. Dacque knows the name of the spirit but I am not sure you do, Dani?"

"Zianos?"

"I guess you do. I found the second one very interesting. I was incarnated with Chief Powhatan in the early days of the settling of Jamestown."

"Neat," Dani commented.

"Now, the third one was a little strange. Not the scene I talked about itself but the fact that the only person I could identify was Mary Santini, who I only met a week ago, and to make it even more confusing she was a man."

Dacque grinned. "That comes up now and then. It is a pretty popular belief that at least most of us experience incarnations as males and females, as well as most of the original five races. It is supposedly a part of our soul development to experience many varied lifetimes."

"Okay, that makes more sense now. So why would the only person I could identify be someone I just met?"

"That one is going to take a little more explaining," Dacque said. "Apparently our souls are part of a soul group that incarnates together more than once, but not always altogether, in order to work on past Karma from previous lives together. Mary came down here after some difficult years experienced back in New York State. None of us knew her three months ago. A number of weeks back, Mary had her first reincarnation session with Eye and identified past lives with members of the family she is now living with two blocks from your house, and also with me in a totally different lifetime. What this means is that we are all pretty much part of the same soul group, and before this round of incarnations our soul group created a basic plan for this lifetime in order to take care of as much past Karmic responsibilities as possible. Mary's coming into our lives here in the city of Anywhere was all preplanned and she will probably play a significant role in our future activities. Hopefully, that makes some sense?"

Carson chuckled. "Some, I guess. I know I do not understand it all, but your explanation helps, and I thank you for that."

"You are welcome."

"I guess I should get home and fill Connie in on how my session went. Are you visiting with Cammi today?"

"Yes, if that is okay?"

"As far as I know it is. Usual time?"

"Usual time. One more thing before you depart. Please tell me a key name or location from your past lifetime with Mary and I will check with her to see if she uncovered it. She did have an incarnation as a man. I know details about two of her three revealed past lives but not the third one."

"Tell her Charlemagne. Are you going to bring her with you to our place today?"

"I can ask her if you like?"

"Probably a good idea. The better Cammi gets to know her, before the first time Mary babysits for us, the less likely there will be a problem."

"I will call Mary and see if she has any plans for this afternoon."

19

Mary rang the doorbell at the Cantland residence a few minutes before two o'clock on Saturday afternoon. Dacque stood to her right but a step behind her with a hand tucked behind his back to conceal Cammi's afternoon surprise.

Cammi opened the door with a wide grin. "Hi, Mary. Hello, Mr. LaRose. Come in please."

Dacque followed Mary into the foyer and closed the door behind him before handing Cammi the gift wrapped in white paper this time.

"Thank you, Mr. LaRose. Mommy and Daddy are waiting for us in the living room," Cammi said, and led the parade into the living room. After greetings all around Cammi asked Connie if she could open her present.

"Yes, honey, you can open it."

Cammi tore the wrapping paper off and checked the book cover. "The Moving Van Next Door."

"And what do you say?" Connie prompted.

"Thank you, Mr. LaRose."

"You are welcome. Shall we sit on the sofa so Mary and I can read the story to you like we did last week?"

Cammi handed Dacque the book and climbed up onto the sofa. Dacque and Mary migrated to the same locations as the week before and Dacque commenced to read the story. "Mary's turn," he said as he reached the approximate mid-point of the storybook and handed it to Mary.

Mary finished reading the story. "Have you ever watched out your window as the movers unloaded a moving van at one of your neighbor's homes?"

"No," Cammi replied.

Mary looked over at Connie.

"It is true. We are apparently the most recent arrivals here amongst those around us. We have only lived here three years this past summer."

"Are you going to come to my room again and read me some more stories?" Cammi asked Mary.

"Would you like me to do that?"

"Yes please."

"Okay, let's do it." Cammi and Mary disappeared down the hallway, leaving the others in silence until it was apparent that Cammi and Mary were well out of hearing range."

"Carson was pretty amazed at the information he provided this morning during his regression session," Connie said. "It was nice that the scene with our Amendola family was much happier than the one I experienced. Of course, we have not had an opportunity to listen to each other's CDs, but we will try to sneak that in one evening soon, after Cammi goes to sleep."

"Did you ask Mary about a Charlemagne incarnation?" Carson asked.

"Yes. That one was the third past lifetime that she revealed, as I expected."

"Great. So, we can listen to our two CDs together like you and Connie and Mary did last Saturday?"

"You certainly can. If you would like, the two of you can get together at my place next Saturday. I hesitate to ask Mary to designate an evening in case she ends up with a lot of homework on that particular day. It seems easier for her to plan activities ahead for the weekends."

"That's fine with me," Carson said. "I have more opportunities to do things like that on the weekends, as well. We can check it out with Mary when she is finished reading stories to Cammi."

Mary read Cammi another four stories on this occasion and quickly departed for the living room as she too was eager to determine if she and Carson discovered a similar event or location in their scenes described for Eyeonthepast while they were hypnotized. The fact that Carson identified her as being there was definitely a good sign, but they could have worked there in the castle together for twenty or thirty years so there were probably thousands of possible situations he could have described. Mary sat down in her spot on the sofa.

"Were your ears ringing?" Carson asked.

Mary gave him a strange glance.

"We were just talking about you and then you appear out of nowhere."

Mary smiled. "I understand. Were you talking about our incarnations with Charlemagne?"

"Amongst other things," Carson replied with a grin.

"Don't let him get you going, Mary. He loves to tease us girls," Connie advised.

"As a matter of fact, we were really only talking about our incarnations with Charlemagne. My scene was the day after he had passed away," Carson said.

"Actually, that was mine too," Mary added.

"Dacque suggested we might get together at his apartment this coming Saturday and have a Charlemagne reunion. Are you interested?"

"Definitely. I found the first reunion with Gramps, err, Mr. LaRose and Connie very interesting. I am really looking forward to the next one."

"Great. Since you live two blocks away from us, I can pick you up and drive you over to Dacque's place instead of him running back and forth. Then I will know where to pick you up when we need you to babysit."

"I'm okay with that. Have you set a time?"

"Dacque," Carson said, "it is your place; what time would you like us?"

"Whatever you two prefer. I walk with Dani on most Saturday mornings, but you all know that we can walk anywhere so you two work out the time."

"I get up early Monday to Friday for school so anytime is good for me," Mary added.

"How about you three settle for nine o'clock?" Connie commented. "That way everyone has most of the day left to do other things."

And nine o'clock it was.

20

Connie advised Carson on Sunday morning, before they climbed out of bed, that after lunch he was taking Cammi to the subdivision's childrens' playground for an hour or so, so that she could sit in Cammi's room and try to make contact with the spirit of Zianos. Carson did not argue.

With Cammi and Carson out the door and on their way to the playground, Connie checked herself in the mirror for the tenth time and nervously headed for Cammi's bedroom. She had no idea where she should situate herself but finally concluded that since Zianos apparently appeared to Cammi at the age of his passing, then she should not be standing but instead down more to his level. She decided to sit on the floor, leaning her back against the side of Cammi's bed, and facing the child's table and chair set over against the wall where Cammi enjoyed tea with her dolls and at times with Zianos. She was certainly interested in hearing any information Cammi shared about her visitor but tried not to alarm her daughter by asking prying questions so her information on their activities in the room was rather sketchy.

"Zianos, are you here? It is your twin sister, Zara. I know I do not look like Zara, but Zara's soul is in my body. That may not make any sense to you, but it is true. I would love to see you and talk to you again. You cannot know how much I missed you after you were ill and how much I even miss you today, as well. If you are here with me, please give me a sign."

Connie figured she had said enough, maybe even too much, so she sat there quietly just looking around the room as the minutes ticked by. She checked behind her at times, and also along the ceiling especially in the corners so that she did not miss any location she could think of, and after the umpteenth check of the circuit she looked again in front of her at the child's table and chair set. Her heart skipped a beat, or more, as she saw the spirit of, she assumed, Zianos, sitting in one chair watching her. "Thank you for visiting with me. You are Zianos, aren't you?"

"Yes."

"You do not know how happy I am to see you again."

"I can imagine."

"I really do not know very much about spirits, so I have only a vague idea of how much you know."

"Way more than you could imagine."

"Oh. Do you know that I used to be your twin sister, Zara?"

"Yes."

"We used to be really close."

"Yes."

"Do you know what I mean by the term, earthbound spirit?"

"Yes."

"Are you an earthbound spirit?"

"No."

"So, you can come and go whenever you like?"

"Yes."

"Do you visit with us often?"

"Yes."

"How long have you been visiting with us here in our house?"

"Since you moved in."

"Oh. How long have you been allowing Cammi to see you?"

"Not very long."

"Why did you suddenly start allowing Cammi to see you?"

"I did not want to frighten her when she was smaller, so I waited for her to grow a little."

"Can you explain why you first showed yourself to Cammi instead of me, your twin sister?"

"She was my mother so we also have a close bond, just like you and I always will. The real reason is that she is only recently departed from the spirit world and still retains some memories from when she was in spirit. As you humans grow older you lose your memory of the time you were in spirit."

"Oh. How do you know all of this?"

"That is a long explanation, and I cannot stay here much longer at this time."

"Why is that?"

"We use up a lot of our energy by materializing so that we can be seen by you humans. These visits need to be rather short."

"I see. Will you talk to me another day?"

"Of course. You are my twin sister," Zianos replied and quickly dematerialized.

"Thank you for visiting with me," Connie called out.

21

Connie did not want to risk sharing with Carson any of the details from her brief conversation with the soul of Zianos when Cammi might overhear their discussion, so she promised she would fill him in on the details after Cammi was asleep in the evening. When their television movie ended at ten o'clock Connie checked Cammi's room and found her sound asleep.

"Out like a light," she advised Carson on her return to the living room.

"Good. Finally. So, how did it go?"

"I decided I would sit on the floor with my back against the side of Cammi's bed and facing her table and chair set. I figured if Zianos visited her as a playmate then his spirit was likely the height he was when he passed away and I did not want to tower over him by standing up."

"Makes sense."

"I then started talking to him, explaining that I was his twin sister even though I did not look like her now, and that we used to be very close. I told him I missed him after he was ill and still miss him, and I would like to talk with him again. After my little spiel I just sat there quietly and regularly looked around the room to see if I could spot anything unusual. I did not check the time but maybe ten minutes later I was doing another visual circuit behind me and along the ceiling, spotting nothing, then I looked in front of me at the table and chair set and there he was sitting in a chair watching me."

"Don't stop now!"

Connie smiled. "At first, I wanted to establish if he was who I thought he was and he confirmed it, as well as his relationship with Cammi and me. We did not get a chance to add you to the conversation but that is on my to-do list."

"It is nice to know that I won't be forgotten in all of the excitement," Carson teased.

"Be good. I want to be serious here. I asked, and Zianos explained, why he appeared first to Cammi instead of me. He said that children retain memories of their time in spirit, but most adults have lost those memories. He has been visiting us since we moved into this house, and maybe even before that but I did not specifically ask him when he began to visit us. He only made contact with Cammi a few months ago because, he explained, that if he tried to do it when she was very young, he might have frightened her."

"Makes sense."

"I did think to ask him if he was an earthbound spirit and he told me no. He visits at will, obviously, but apparently does not stay here all of the time."

"So, we are not haunted?"

"We are not haunted. When I asked him how he knew so much about the spirit world he said that it was a long explanation, and it would have to wait for another time as he needed to go soon. He explained that materializing so we could see him uses up a lot of his energy."

"Interesting. I hope you get a chance to hear about his knowledge of the spirit world."

"He said he would talk with me another day."

"Good. This sounds exciting and there appears to not be any danger in conversing with him."

"I agree."

"When are you going to try to contact him again?"

"I have been thinking about that. If he needs to accumulate more energy to be seen by me then I probably should not try again for a week or so. Certainly not for a few days but we will see when the next opportunity presents itself."

"Makes sense."

22

Carson and Mary arrived at Dacque's apartment a few minutes before nine on Saturday morning for their Charlemagne reunion. They chatted with Dani and Dacque for a few minutes before Dacque and Dani departed on their scheduled walk, allowing the reunion to be commenced with no outside listeners.

"This is my first reunion, as I am sure you know, so I will rely on you to guide me through this as I know this is not your first one," Carson said.

"The process is not much of a big deal, but I will follow the same procedures that we went through during my two, past life reunions, with Mr. LaRose and Connie recently, and an earlier one with all of the Westgates you just met when you picked me up. I was not living with them at the time but was still residing in Mr. LaRose's spare room. There were four of us at the reunion at the Westgates and we listened to the four CDs in the chronological order that our regression sessions took place. It may be obvious, but the reason for listening to them in that order was on the earlier CDs I could not be identified by any of the Westgates because they did not know me at the time of their regression sessions, just like I could not identify you at my session as I did not know you," Mary explained.

"I understand."

"If you have no questions, I will slip my CD into Mr. LaRose's player and we can listen to it."

"Let's listen."

Mary started up the player and settled down on the other end of Dacque's sofa.

"That was very similar to my revelations after the reported death of our beloved Charlemagne. Do you know if it is common or unusual to experience almost similar scenes?" Carson asked.

"It may not be that unusual. In my incarnation with Rosalie and Raluca back a thousand years ago the three of us described the same, rather traumatic scene, at least to us back then. Now you and I have a similar situation with the death of Charlemagne. Do you have any other questions, or shall we listen to your CD now?"

"No more questions."

"You were right," Mary said when the CD stopped, "that was pretty similar to my scene. I was happy to hear you reveal my last name, or really Jean-Louis' last name as Chartrand, which for whatever reason I did not state in my answer to Eye. Other than that, I did not pick out anything else strikingly different between the two CDs. Do you have any idea at all why we would both consider this time of mourning as such a significant event in comparison to other activities that must have taken place at the palace?"

"I did a little research on Charlemagne and it appears that he spent much of his time conquering the world as he knew it, so he likely never had a lot of time to relax in our palace. When he was there, we were kept busy I'm sure, but when he was not there it may have been rather dull around the old palace except when some of his relatives were in residence. My guess is that we were so set in our routines that his death probably abruptly caused us to wonder whether our lives would be drastically changed by it."

"I don't know anything about Charlemagne, really, but what you say makes sense to me."

"I guess if we have no other questions concerning our CDs I had better get back home and do some work before you and Dacque arrive for Cammi's story-time hour."

"I cannot think of any other questions," Mary replied. "We'll see you around two as usual, I gather."

23

Mary and Dacque arrived at the Cantland home around two o'clock on Saturday afternoon. Mary seemed quite happy to join Dacque each week on his visits and he was delighted to have the opportunity to spend much of their Saturdays in the company of his former apartment guest. Dacque contemplated the notion that it would be nice if Mary handed Cammi her storybook gift on this occasion, but in the final analysis he was concerned that if Cammi got used to receiving books from Mary then she might also expect Mary to come baring gifts on the days when she was employed as their babysitter, so he scrapped the whole idea. Mary rang the doorbell.

Cammi welcomed her expected visitors, accepted Dacque's package in pink wrapping paper, and then escorted them into the living room where Carson and Connie were awaiting them. After greetings all around, Cammi asked Connie if she could open her gift.

"Of course, honey. Mr. LaRose brings it for you."

Cammi quickly disposed of the wrapping paper and looked at the front cover. "Polly the Parrot," she read out loud.

"Story time as usual?" Dacque asked.

"Yes, Mr. LaRose," Cammi replied. She handed him the book and climbed up onto the center of the sofa. Dacque and Mary migrated to their usual locales and Dacque began to read the new story.

Dacque passed the book over to Mary when he was halfway through and she finished reading it. "Do you know anyone who has a parrot for a pet?" she asked Cammi.

"No. I have a friend with a budgie, but no one has a parrot. Are we going to my room again today to read more of my books?"

"We sure are. Let's go!"

Cammi hopped off of the sofa and ran towards her bedroom with Mary hustling along behind her.

Connie waited until she was sure the coast was clear and turned to Dacque. "I finally managed to have a short chat with Zianos in Cammi's room on Sunday."

"Marvelous. How did it go?"

"I was happy with the information I received. I had hoped our visit would last longer but Zianos claimed that materializing so we can see him uses up extra energy and he could only stay for a short while, and then he disappeared."

"As far as I know, that is correct."

"Good. I figured it was the truth, but I did not consider that our chat would end so soon, and somewhat abruptly."

"I have heard of the low energy problem before in conversations with the spirt of a child I assisted to crossover at the children's hospital. Zianos must be able to determine when his energy is getting low, so he needs to make his exit. How much did you learn?"

"He said he was not earthbound but visits with us whenever he likes. He has been doing it here since we moved into this house three years ago this past summer. I did not think to ask whether he was visiting us at our previous home also. He knew

I was Zara and that Cammi had been his mother. He said he came to her first instead of me because younger children still have some memories of their lives in spirit, but this is lost as they get older."

"As far as I know that is also correct."

"He also said that he waited until recently to allow Cammi to see him because if he did it when she was too young, he might have frightened her."

"That makes sense."

"After he said he needed to go soon I asked if he would visit with me again and he said yes. I am going to chase Carson and Cammi off to the playground tomorrow afternoon, unless something comes up, and try to reach him again."

"Good."

"Can you think of anything in particular that I should ask or say?"

"You seem to be doing quite well on your own. Your conscious mind may not realize it but your soul mind, the soul of his twin, Zara, may be connecting with Zianos and prompting you as you contemplate your questions. The best advice I can give you is to ask whatever comes into your mind because you may be guided from inside you."

"Interesting. Thank you, I will remember that. Maybe we should change the topic of our conversation now before Mary returns. I gather she does not know much about this?"

"Only whatever you have told her."

24

With Carson and Cammi off to the neighborhood playground for an hour or so, Connie settled down on the floor in Cammi's room with her back resting against her daughter's bed, just like the previous week. "Hello, Zianos. Are you present in our house today?" Connie dispensed with her long spiel from the first week and sat there waiting in silence. She did not bother scouring the room with her eyes as she had the past Sunday, assuming that if Zianos was going to appear to her he would do so again over at Cammi's table and chairs set. This time the wait seemed much shorter and was certainly more thrilling as she was able to witness the spirit of Zianos materialize in front of her eyes, upon the same chair he appeared on the week before. Connie grinned from ear to ear. "I am honored to have the opportunity to watch you materialize for me this week. Thank you very much for that."

"You are very welcome."

"Do you have anything in particular that you would like to ask or tell me this visit, or shall I do the asking?"

"There are many things I could tell you but for now it is

probably best if you asked some questions that you are curious about."

"Okay. How old were you when you passed on into spirit?"

"Six."

"Are you conversing with me as a six-year-old?"

"Do I sound like a six-year-old?"

"No, you really don't. You talk as if you were an adult, I think. Can you explain that?"

"A soul remembers everything it experiences, from all of its lifetimes incarnated on the earth and also everything it experiences while in spirit, like my conversations with you. Your human memory will forget some of the details of the things we talk about, over time, unless you write them down, but I will remember everything for eternity."

"So, you know everything that has ever happened, everywhere?"

"No. The key word is experienced. I will have no memory of anything Carson and Cammi do or say at the park today unless I zip over there and listen and watch. See the difference?"

"Yes, thank you for clarifying that. Can you explain the reason or reasons you spend a lot of time in our home?"

"Does that bother you?"

"No, no. Do not get that impression. I am seeking to understand the purpose of your time spent with us when you could be anyplace you like, I presume?"

"Yes, I could be anyplace I like, that is true. I am still very connected to the souls of your family because of our lives together as the Amendola family, and we are all part of the same larger soul group that is working on Karma and relationships from our past lives together."

"You mean we have shared more than one past life together?"

"Oh yes."

"I would love to hear about those other past lives."

"That is one thing that I should not reveal to you. You first need to discover those past lives before I talk to you about them."

"Why is that?"

"Think experience, again. Your soul knows everything you experienced, everywhere. I only know about the things in your past lives that I experienced while with you or talking to you and that is far less than your total experiences in any other lifetime with me. I am not trying to cut off this discussion, and you can bring it up again, but my energy is waning, and I must leave you for now."

"Thank you for coming," Connie shouted as the spirit of Zianos faded away.

25

Connie checked Cammi's room at nine in the evening to confirm that her daughter was sound asleep and then returned to the living room where Carson was eagerly awaiting his updates from her afternoon visit with Zianos. "Sound asleep."

"Good."

"This afternoon was another, shorter-than-I would-have-liked visit with him but he needed to disappear when his energy level was depleting."

"I guess you just have to get used to that fact and be selective in what you two talk about."

"It looks like it, but it never seems long enough."

"I understand. So, what exciting news did you learn this time?"

"First, he confirmed that he died at age six."

"Did he seem upset about that?"

"No, not really. He then explained that souls remember everything that they experience in all of their incarnations as well as their time spent in spirit. As an example, he said he would remember everything we chatted about but would know nothing about your time at the playground with Cammi unless he popped over there to watch you."

"That makes sense to me."

"He does spend a lot of time at our house because of our previous connection in the Amendola family and we are also all part of the same soul group."

"That makes sense, too."

"He shocked me near the end when he said that he and I experienced other incarnations together as well as the Amendola one."

"That sounds interesting. What did he tell you?"

"Nothing, unfortunately. He explained that he only knew the pieces of other incarnations with me, or anyone for that matter, that he personally experienced, whereas I know, or my soul knows, everything about all of my other incarnations so it is best that I discover these other incarnations before we talk about them."

"Oh. I guess that makes sense. Are you going to request another session with Eyeonthepast?"

"Probably, but maybe not right away. Right now, I want to quiz Zianos all that I can because who knows when he might stop chatting with me."

"Sounds reasonable."

"Are you interested in joining me sometime when I have a chat with him?"

"Do you think he will visit with you if I am there?"

"Probably. You were his father. I figured I would ask him if it was okay before I did it, anyway."

"Okay, I would love to join you but exactly how are we going to pull this off when we need one of us to watch Cammi?"

"She told me the other day that a friend at school was going to invite her to her birthday party this Saturday. The invitations are supposed to be handed out in a day or two. I hope to try to visit with Zianos after dinner one day soon on a nice evening when you can take Cammi to the playground. I was meaning to ask Zianos today if I could bring you along on one of my visits, but he pulled his disappearing act before I got a chance to ask. If necessary, we could ask Mary to babysit for an hour or two on a Saturday or Sunday and take her to the playground while we visited with Zianos. I feel bad that after asking Mary if she would be our new babysitter, we have not needed her services yet."

"Okay, you make it work and I will be happy to visit with Zianos."

26

The weather was warm and sunny on Wednesday evening, absolutely perfect for an after-dinner excursion for Cammi and Carson to the playground. Connie texted her husband from the parking garage after work to let him know that she planned to feed them frozen pizzas for dinner, and then shoo them off to the park so she could attempt to contact Zianos for a third time. Connie hustled her family out the door and on their way to the playground by a couple of minutes after six. She quickly loaded the dinner dishes in the dishwasher and headed for Cammi's bedroom.

"Zianos, are you here this evening? I know it is only four days since we last chatted, but you never did tell me how long of a time you required to regain your energy level so you could materialize again." Connie sat quietly in her usual spot on the floor, leaning against the side of her daughter's bed, and watched the table and chair set in front of her. Within minutes she smiled from ear to ear once more as she eagerly observed her former twin brother materialize on his favorite chair. "Thank you for visiting again, and for allowing me to witness your materialization."

"You are welcome, of course."

"Thank you. How long do you need to wait before allowing me to see you again?"

"Generally, two days should be fine, but it does take longer when my energy has been practically depleted, kind of like your techie gadgets in your world."

Connie smiled. "Thank you. One more out-of-the-blue question – is it alright if I invite Carson to join us in our chats? Do you know he was your father?"

"Yes, on both counts."

"Thank you. Do you have anything you wish to tell me or ask me?"

"Not for now. You ask the questions."

"Okay. As you know, Carson, Cammi and I were all with you in your previous life. Have you had another incarnation since you were Zianos?"

"No."

"How come you have not reincarnated with the three of us in our current lifetime?"

"That is not a simple explanation. The primary, but not only, reason for the incarnations a soul chooses is to advance the development of our soul. To give you a generalized answer, the appropriate body for my next incarnation has not come into existence as of yet."

"Will it eventually be in our Cantland family, somewhere?"

"Possibly, maybe even probably, but there are other options in different families where I have experienced past-life connections, and it is possible that my most advantageous next incarnation could be in one of those families."

"I thought a lot of things were preplanned within our soul group before we were all incarnated. Is that correct?"

"Yes, but the preplanning usually includes at least a few options, because the free will possessed by humans and also by souls will sometimes mess up our preplanning."

"I understand. That does make sense."

"Good."

"So, you have revealed that you spend a lot of time here in our home. Do you do the same in other homes where you might incarnate?"

"Yes, and also elsewhere with past soul connections even though I am unlikely to incarnate soon with them in body."

"Why bother if you are not likely to incarnate with them in your next body?"

"Think of it as friends. I am interested in knowing how their current lives are progressing this time around. Remember, anything I witness, or experience, becomes part of my soul memory and this knowledge may be a factor in my choosing a future family down the road."

"I see. How is your energy level holding up?"

"It is getting low."

"Okay. Cammi is invited to a friend's birthday party on Saturday afternoon. I hope to visit with you then and bring Carson along. Will that work with your schedule?"

"I will make it work. Goodbye for now," Zianos said and commenced to dematerialize before Connie's eyes.

27

Connie checked in on Cammi at nine o'clock and concluded that she was sound asleep. "I want to phone Dacque to let him know that Cammi will be attending the birthday party on Saturday afternoon so he and Mary can make other plans for the afternoon if they so desire," she advised Carson. "I will also bring him up to date on the last two visits I had with Zianos as I'm sure he is eager to hear about them. If you listen in, and I know you will, then we can talk about anything you like when I get off of the phone, okay?"

"That is fine."

Connie dialed Dacque's apartment.

"Hello."

"Hi, Dacque, it's Connie. I hope I am not catching you at a bad time?"

"Not at all."

"Good. I wanted to update you on a couple of things. First, Cammi has been invited to a friend's birthday party on Saturday afternoon so you get a Saturday afternoon off from story time."

Dacque chuckled. "I'm sure I can find something to do."

"I am sure you can. Secondly, I have experienced two further visits with Zianos, and I believe our visits have been progressing rather nicely. I will give you the highlights in a minute, but I want to make sure I do not forget to inform you that I asked Zianos if I could invite Carson along on our chat while Cammi is attending the birthday party and he said sure."

"That is great. I'm certain he will find it interesting."

"He is pretty excited about it. Okay, here is some of the information Zianos has shared with me on the past two visits." Connie glanced down at the notes that she faithfully recorded after each visit with her former twin brother. "He confirmed that he was only six when he passed over and did not appear to sound emotional about it."

"I do not think souls on the other side are emotional. I suspect that is a human characteristic."

"He explained that souls remember everything they experience in body and in spirit, but you probably already know that?"

"Yes, I do."

"I was excited to hear that Zianos and I shared other past lives together but disappointed that he would not give me any details. He did explain why."

"You have to discover those past lives first?"

"Yes."

"I've heard it before."

"I figured you would have," Connie stated. "I asked and he confirmed that he has not incarnated again after his life as Zianos. He went on to explain that he may incarnate into our family sometime in the future if the appropriate opportunity arises, but he also has at least one other situation where he could join a different family if the right opportunity opened up there. I questioned him on the belief that our soul group preplanned at least some of our current lives, before we started incarnating, and he said that this planning includes options because free will can interfere with some of the preplanning."

"Wow, you two are getting into some serious discussions. That is wonderful news. I have heard about the options and free will problems before, but I am a little surprised it came up so soon in your chats with him."

"I have been trying to ask for explanations and not just facts, so I suspect that I encouraged it."

"Super. Keep it up."

"Oh, I plan on it. That is pretty much the highlights of our two recent chats. Seeing as Zianos did not balk at allowing Carson to join our next conversation, if you are interested, would you like me to inquire whether I can invite you to join us some time? It is strange how this adventure has taken a different direction than what we suspected when Dani first put me in contact with you. We figured that you would be the one to try to contact Zianos and here I am asking if you would like to join us."

"You have learned a lot in a few weeks, and you were certainly the best one of us to attempt to make first contact with him."

"You prepared me for the challenge extremely well and I sincerely thank you for that."

"You are most welcome. I look forward to my next update and certainly welcome the opportunity to talk with Zianos if I get the chance."

"Talk to you soon. Bye for now."

"Bye."

28

Connie dropped Cammi off at the birthday party a few minutes before two on Saturday afternoon and excitedly hurried home to Carson. She settled down in her usual spot on the floor in Cammi's room facing the table and chair set. Carson eased his much larger frame down on the floor beside her.

"You can sit on her bed if it is more comfortable," Connie suggested.

"I'm down here now so I might as well stay here."

"If you become uncomfortable just quietly get up and sit on the bed. I do not think any gentle movement will scare him off."

"Okay, I'll do that."

Connie and Carson sat there in silence for a minute before Connie commenced to converse with Zianos. "Hello Zianos. Are you here with us today?" Connie previously coached Carson to keep his eyes on the table and chair set so he would catch Zianos materializing on a chair. Within a minute the eagerly anticipated event commenced. Connie glanced quickly at Carson to observe his reaction and he appeared to her to be in a trance-like state, staring straight ahead at the miracle occurring in front of them. "Thank you for joining us today," Connie said after Zianos was fully materialized.

"You are welcome, as usual."

"Thank you. As you can see, I brought along Carson, today."

"Hello Dad."

Caught totally by surprise, Carson choked noticeably on his words. "Hello ... son. You cannot imagine how wonderful it is to see you again."

"I can sort of imagine your excitement from my experiences while incarnated but I have the distinct advantage of seeing you often when I visit your home, so the shock effect does not exist for me."

"I understand."

"Do you have any recollections of our life together?" Zianos asked.

Carson paused before responding. "I did not think that I did but seeing you again now I appear to be remembering some events from back then, especially when you were ill."

"It is not surprising. As Zara has already told you, your soul knows everything you experienced from your lifetime as Italo and in special moments like this your soul may be releasing glimpses of the past into your conscious mind."

"That is interesting. I hope it continues."

"It probably will. The more you believe that you are able to receive information from your soul mind the more likely you will recognize it as it happens and not sluff it off as imagination."

"Wow, I had no idea that it worked that way."

"Unfortunately, most humans are so wrapped up in human activities they have lost contact with their soul mind, if they even know it exists."

"You are privy to an amazing amount of information."

"Humans remember some of their life experiences. Souls remember all of their experiences from all of their incarnations, as well as their time here in the in-between. We have a major advantage over you."

"That is apparent. Zara told me that you and she experienced other lifetimes together before our Amendola one. Did you and I also experience other lifetimes together?"

"Yes."

"Was that the same lifetime with the three of us together or totally different lifetimes for Zara's and my soul?"

"Both."

"Both! That is interesting. What about Cammi's soul?"

"Both."

"So, we incarnate together at times and separately at times?"

"Yes."

"I would love an explanation, so I have a better understanding of all of this."

"We are all part of the same soul group, but this soul group includes many other souls. We incarnate together, not necessarily all four of us sometimes, but we also incarnate with different souls at other times. It is basically determined by Karma, and our soul's required journey through experiences for our soul's progress in development. Some incarnations provide ideal situations for major soul progress but other times we incarnate primarily to assist other souls with their progress, even though we may not benefit that much ourselves. In brief, kindness is a miracle for development in both your world and here on this side."

"Amazing! That certainly throws a new perspective on the human purpose of life."

"If only more humans understood this it would be a much safer world you exist in."

"How is your energy level holding out?" Connie asked.

"It is getting low."

"Before you go, I need to ask you a question. Are you

familiar with a nice man who has been visiting with us often on Saturday afternoons, by the name of Dacque LaRose?"

"Yes."

"He knows much more about souls than we do and would love to visit with you sometime if that is alright with you?"

"Of course. We have spent lifetimes together."

"You have? He will love to hear that."

"We are all part of the same soul group, remember?"

"Yes, that makes sense, but I am learning so much from both you and Dacque that I do not always keep all of the information straight."

"I know. Bye for now."

"Bye."

Connie and Carson watched as the spirit of Zianos became lighter and lighter and finally disappeared.

"Well, what did you think?" Connie asked.

"I wouldn't have missed it for the world."

29

Connie dialed Dacque's number.

"Hello."

"Hi Dacque, it's Connie. I was unsure whether you would be home on your Saturday off from reading story books to six-year-olds."

Dacque chuckled. "I had Mary over this morning, and she stayed for lunch, but I just returned from driving her home. She is all excited; she has a date tonight, her first at her new school."

"That is marvelous. I hope she has a super time. Carson and I just wrapped up our visit with Zianos. It was very informative. Zianos spent most of his time talking with Carson, which was fine with me. Zianos explained a lot of things about souls and soul groups and why souls select certain incarnations. He concluded that topic with the declaration that kindness was the miracle for soul development during incarnations as well as while in spirit."

"Yes. The secret that so few people are aware of. It is sad."

"I asked Zianos, before he ran out of energy, whether you could visit with him sometime and he said of course. He then shocked me by declaring that he shared incarnations with you as well. I should not have been so shocked, but he just caught me by surprise, I guess. He reminded me that we are all part of the same soul group, so it made perfect sense, after I had time to digest the information. A rookie's mistake, I guess."

"We were all rookies at one point. Did he happen to give you a clue as to our incarnations together? Of course, I had no way of identifying him when I had my regression sessions with Eyeonthepast."

"No. No clue and he was running low on energy, so I did not think to ask him. Another rookie mistake."

"No problem. I will ask him when I visit with him. Do you have any idea when that might take place?"

"On a nice evening, I can send Cammi and Carson off to the playground after dinner. I could give you a call as soon as they leave if we have not prearranged it ahead of time. Can you usually react instantly if I suddenly phone you out of the blue?"

"I live alone, as you know, so I can be there in fifteen minutes on most evenings."

"And if you are in the middle of dinner?"

"My microwave works just fine. I'm a pro, not a rookie."

Connie laughed. "I will call you next week first chance we can pull this off. If we cannot make it work on an evening, then maybe Saturday afternoon will be our rain day. Bye for now."

"Bye."

30

It was Thursday evening before their schedules and the weather coordinated to allow Carson and Cammi to truck off to the playground after dinner. True to his word, Dacque was on Connie's doorstep within fifteen minutes.

Connie settled into her usual spot on the floor facing the table and chair set, with her back against the side of Cammi's bed. Dacque opted for sitting on the bed instead of the floor.

"Hello Zianos. Are you visiting with us this evening?" Within two minutes, the spirit of Zianos commenced to materialize on his apparently favorite chair. "Thank you for joining us this evening," Connie said. "As you can see, we have a new guest tonight."

"Hello, Dacque."

"Hello, Zianos. Nice to meet you. Thank you for agreeing to allow me to visit with you and Connie."

"You are welcome. I have been eagerly waiting for an opportunity to chat with you sometime."

"You have?"

"That's right. We have experienced some interesting past life connections."

"I am glad to hear that. Do you hang around my apartment at times like you do here at the Cantland's home?"

"Oh, yes. Often."

"Why have you not made your presence felt while you are there?"

"I was waiting for Zara to introduce us."

"Was that really necessary?"

"No, but more desirable. I know you have talked with a few spirits in the past but think about it; you either knew them in your current lifetime or went looking for them at the children's hospital. Even if I appeared to you as I looked when we were incarnated together in the past, you would not recognize me. I doubt that I would have scared you if I suddenly appeared in your apartment, but it was better to wait until Zara brought us together. That is how we preplanned it."

"Nice to see the plan is working."

"I agree."

"So, what can you tell me about our past lives together?"

"You have only uncovered one of our past lives together in your regression sessions so that is all we can talk about."

"And which one was that?"

"The one with Ra-Ta."

"Oh, that was an interesting one. And who were you?"

"I think it is best if you went home and listened to that CD again, to refresh your memory on the details from that lifetime. You have not listened to that CD for a while, at least whenever I was hanging around."

"You are correct on that point. Does it make sense that you visit with me at my apartment and we listen to it together?"

"That makes good sense."

"When should we schedule that?"

"If I do not use up too much energy today, we can do it tomorrow afternoon or evening. Zara, do you have anything you wish to chat about today?"

"Nothing that cannot wait until another time so you can leave us early if you wish."

"Okay, I will do that. Dacque, I will look in on you from three o'clock on, your time, tomorrow afternoon at your apartment. If you are out or busy, I will hang around or check in on you regularly until you are available."

"That sounds good. I look forward to your visit."

"Me, also," Zianos replied and proceeded to dematerialize.

After Zianos disappeared, Connie got up off of the floor and sat on the bed along with Dacque. "What did he mean when he said from three o'clock on, your time?" she asked.

"Apparently time is a human activity, probably tied into the human aging process. All indications seem to imply that time means nothing on the other side. Souls and spirits do not age. They can be there a thousand years and look the same if they never incarnated."

"Then how does he know when three o'clock tomorrow afternoon arrives?"

"I assume by observing us and our surroundings. He can look at clocks or our watches or our computers when they are on. He can notice sunsets and sunrises, so he knows when days change. He probably has the ability to research just about anything in our world where he can locate information on the subject."

"Can he read books that are closed?"

"You've got me on that one. I have absolutely no idea."

31

Dacque was prepared for his visit with Zianos before two forty-five on Friday afternoon and almost counted the seconds as he waited in his easy chair for the spirit to reveal itself. The wait was short-lived. He spotted the spirit materializing on the sofa near him. "Welcome to my humble abode."

"Thank you. I have been here many times before, but it is nice to finally be able to reveal my presence to you and speak with you."

"I second that motion. Are we ready to listen to the CD from my early incarnation with Ra-Ta?"

"I'm ready if you are."

Dacque walked over to the CD player in his entertainment center and pressed the play button.

"I would now like you to once again," Eyeonthepast's voice came through loud and clear, "picture yourself back in the gently sloping tunnel you were in previously, sliding slowly along towards the light at the bottom. When you exit from the tunnel this time you will land into a previous lifetime other than the one as Henri Lafromboise. Please tell me when you are out of the tunnel."

"I am out of the tunnel."

"Please tell me what you see or what you are doing."

"We are all preparing to leave our temporary home here in the Nubian lands and return to our homes in the Egyptian lands."

"When you refer to all of you, how many do you mean?"

"Over two hundred."

"Please explain why you are returning home to the Egyptian lands."

"Our leader, the High Priest Ra-Ta, has been invited to return to our homeland after his banishment over a decade ago."

"Do you know the reason he was banished?"

"Yes. He broke his own rule of taking only one woman and King Araaraart, his friend, was pressured by Ra-Ta's detractors into banishing him for his transgressions."

"Are you aware of why Ra-Ta is now being welcomed back to the Egyptian lands?"

"The messenger said that Ra-Ta's work in developing the perfect society was in chaos and he needed to return to remedy this demise."

"I see. What is your name?"

"Ragestan."

"Are you a relative of Ra-Ta's?"

"No."

"Were you banished from the Egyptian lands?"

"No."

"Why did you leave the Egyptian lands with Ra-Ta?"

"I was one of his friends and dedicated assistants in the Temple Beautiful and decided my family should leave with him instead of remain in the Temple without our gifted leader."

"Tell me about your family."

"My woman and best friend is Nandemondu. We have two daughters, Landemondu and Randemondu."

"Was your family not upset about leaving the Egyptian lands?"

"They were upset about leaving their friends and relatives behind but many of our close relatives came with us. My family had witnessed the unique gifts possessed by Ra-Ta and understood why our place was to follow him."

"Tell me about the Temple Beautiful."

"The purpose of the Temple Beautiful was to evaluate individuals and determine their greatest qualities. Then we would train them to use these gifts for the benefit of creating the perfect society."

"Did it work?"

"It was a long-term goal. There was definite progress achieved while I was alive."

"I see. Can you give me an example or two of the work performed in the Temple Beautiful?"

"An individual with high technical aptitude would be trained as a technical specialist. Men and women with high intelligence would be bred together to produce superior children."

"Were the local people forced to participate in the activities in the Temple Beautiful?"

"No. It was voluntary, but they were awarded perks for participating."

"What kind of perks?"

"Free education and training. The individuals who agreed to participate in the superior breeding program were provided with luxurious accommodations."

"Interesting. I would now like you to look around at the people you knew back in your lifetime as Ragestan and see if any of them are or have been incarnated with you in your current lifetime. If so, please identify them in both lifetimes."

"Nandemondu was my late wife, Beverly. Randemondu was Beverly's mother Bonita Tarasenko."

"Thank you for that information."

32

Dacque looked over at the spirit of Zianos. "That definitely has to be one on my most interesting past lives."

"Mine also. Those were amazing times," the spirit replied.

"Where did you fit in to the story?"

"I was your brother Dagestan. My family accompanied your family and the others to the Nubian lands with Ra-Ta. I also worked in the Temple Beautiful but not directly with you. You were involved in the testing of the individuals to determine the vocations that they were best suited for. I was a teacher in the agricultural production division."

"That's interesting. Exactly what was the Temple Beautiful?"

"The best way I can describe it is like a university today but where the students or entrants are first tested to determine their aptitudes and then placed in the program that they are most suited for. Not all entrants were thrilled with the testing results because they had a greater personal interest in other fields, but your department was quite skilled in persuading them that it was not only best for their future but also the perfect society if they entered an occupation that they were best suited for. Most of them eventually agreed but a few would leave the program."

"How do you know so much about universities today? They probably did not even have universities during your incarnation before Zianos."

"Have you ever been over to The University of Anywhere?"

"Actually, no."

"I pop over there often and sit in on interesting courses or lectures. Unseen, of course."

"Fantastic. So, you probably know as much about today's society as we do simply by selectively observing us?"

"Right on, man. I can even talk the lingo."

Dacque laughed. "That's hilarious. What else can you tell me about our time together in the Nubian and Egyptian lands?"

"Well, both of your daughters went through the Temple Beautiful program, as did my three children. Landemondu was very creative and exceptionally bright. She was trained in architecture and was bred to one of the Atlantean migrants. Many of the Atlanteans were amazingly intelligent. Their technological abilities in some areas exceeded the technical knowledge in your world today."

"I have read about the Atlantean technological abilities. It definitely was amazing."

"Some of their brightest minds migrated to our Egyptian lands when they were warned that their remaining islands would soon disappear into the ocean. Some of them worked with us in the Temple Beautiful."

"How about Randemondu?"

"She was more suited to the technological studies. She fell in love with one of her Atlantean technical instructors. Their marriage was approved because of their high levels of intelligence. I hate to cut you off while we are into some interesting topics of discussion but my energy level is getting low so I must disappear."

"I understand. Will we chat again?"

"Of course. Now that you actually know me, I can make myself seen when I visit you," Zianos advised and commenced to dematerialize.

33

On Thursday evening, after Connie and Dacque's conversation with the spirit of Zianos in Cammi's bedroom, they agreed that they would resume Dacque and Mary's story time with Cammi on Saturday afternoon. Mary rang the doorbell while Dacque faithfully hid Cammi's new storybook behind his back, even though after so many story-time afternoons a gift was no longer much of a surprise, its contents always excited her.

"Hello Mary. Hello Mr. LaRose," Cammi greeted her visitors after she opened the door.

Dacque handed Cammi her gift in the foyer and she escorted their company into the living room where greetings were exchanged all around. "May I open it now, Mommy?" Cammi inquired.

"Of course, Dear," Connie responded.

Cammi quickly removed the white wrapping paper and checked the cover. "Puddle jumping," she read with a giggle. "This one looks like fun. Are you going to read it to me, Mr. LaRose?"

"Of course, Mary and I would love to read it to you."

Cammi handed Dacque the storybook and climbed up in the middle of the sofa. Mary and Dacque joined her. When he was approximately halfway through the story Dacque passed the book over to Mary. "Do you ever go puddle jumping?" Mary asked Cammi when she completed reading the story.

Cammi glanced hesitantly at her mother before she responded. "Sometimes," she grudgingly conceded.

Everyone enjoyed a good chuckle before Cammi and Mary took off for Cammi's bedroom for part two of story-time afternoon.

The living room fell silent until Connie was convinced that Mary and Cammi were secure in Cammi's bedroom. "I can't wait to hear about your reaction to listening to your Ra-Ta CD again with Zianos' spirit. Having a spirit present while listening to a past lifetime; is that a new experience?"

"Definitely, but a very rewarding one. Zianos was able to supply a lot of interesting information about our lives together, probably thousands of years ago in early Egypt. We were brothers in that lifetime. I am sorry that I cannot share with you any details because it is still possible that you or Carson or even both of you were with us in that incarnation."

"We understand," Connie assured him.

"After being materialized while we listened to the CD, Zianos and I did not have a lot of time to talk about those times as his energy was depleting. He promised to visit me again, so I am eager to continue our discussion."

"I'll bet you are. Carson and I have decided we will have a second past life regression with Eyeonthepast where we will each specify we would like information on other lives we shared with Zianos. Is that a proper request?"

"I believe so. It might be more appropriate to just request that you visit one other significant previous lifetime with Zianos' spirit, because there might not even have been three of them."

"Good point. We emailed Eyeonthepast for one spot this coming Saturday morning and another on the Saturday after that. Is it alright if we use your apartment again?"

"Certainly. Just let me know what your timeslot is when you hear from Eye and I will schedule my walks with Dani around them."

"Thank you, we will do that."

"Are you going to attempt to contact Zianos again tomorrow afternoon?"

"I hope so. Do you think he will have his battery recharged by then?"

"Probably. It will be almost forty-eight hours so he should be okay even if he has to cut your visit short."

"Good. How does he know where to be at times when he has so many places that he visits?"

"I have been told by a different spirit that they can pop off anywhere, basically instantly, so he could pop into your place for a few seconds and determine what is going on and then move on elsewhere to check out other locations. With his infallible memory he also knows which particular locations are prime for a visit by him on any particular day or time. He would know what days and times you would likely be home and not even check up on you through the week when you are working."

"That makes sense."

34

With Carson and Cammi off to the playground after lunch on Sunday, Connie tidied up the dishes and settled down in her regular location in Cammi's bedroom for another visit with the spirit of her former twin brother. "Hello Zianos. Are you around today?" She waited less than a minute before she observed his spirit materializing on the chair to the right of Cammi's table that he habitually appeared on. "Thank you for coming again today."

"You are welcome. I suspect that I look forward to our visits as much as you do."

"I am sincerely thrilled to hear you say that. Dacque told me that you two experienced an interesting visit at his apartment on Friday, even though you could not talk with him for very long after you listened to his CD."

"Yes, it was exciting for me to be able to chat with him about that memorable lifetime we shared in early Egypt. I plan to return one day this week, hopefully, and continue our discussion."

"While we are speaking about Dacque, are you always here

in our house when he comes for story time with Cammi on Saturday afternoons?"

"I have certainly been here for many of them but if I missed any then I might not have known they were to take place."

"I see. So, you do not specifically plan to be here for them?"

"Well, sort of. Because I visit many locations, I can sometimes remain longer in some instances than I initially expected to, especially if something interesting is going on in those locations. But I have not experienced any instances where I knew about Dacque's pending visit with Cammi and was delayed, so if I missed any then I was not aware that they were scheduled."

"I understand. Were you here yesterday when I told Dacque that Carson and I were scheduling another regression session with Eyeonthepast and we planned to specifically request we uncover another past lifetime shared with you?"

"Yes."

"Good. Is there any actual way you can give me some information on which incarnation that I should try to search out?"

"I think I know which one you will uncover but I should not influence that decision. I suggest that you ask Eyeonthepast to word it something like this. Please lead me to the past lifetime with the spirit I know as Zianos that is most relevant to this lifetime, other than the one I identified in my first regression session. People generally uncover past lives that are significant to their current lifetime, at least in the opinion of their soul, so you should come up with the most significant one."

"Thank you for that important suggestion. Do you really enjoy these chats that you have with the group of us?"

"Oh yes. I can visit basically any place I want in your world, whenever I want to, and the observations become part of my soul memory, as you know, but it is much more exciting when I am able to materialize for folks and converse with them."

"That makes perfect sense. You said you could visit basically any place you wanted in our world. That implies to me that there are places you cannot visit, am I correct?"

"I am not sure that 'cannot' is actually the correct word. Should not is more accurate."

"Okay, explain please."

"It is easy enough to accumulate bad Karma while incarnated so most souls try to avoid adding to that while on the other side. If we encounter situations where we definitely do not belong, then we pop right back out. For example, I would never pop into your bathroom because I have no right or reason to be there. When you and Carson were first married you had the freedom of enjoying sex anytime and anywhere when you were alone. If I popped in to visit you in your living room and you were enjoying that activity, then I would immediately pop back out."

"Did that actually happen?" Connie asked, feeling the heat of her beet-red blush.

"Yes, a few times, but I assure you that I was gone in a second."

"I see. So, if you had of stayed and watched us having a good time then that would have caused you some negative Karma?"

"Yes, just the same as some peeping Tom snooping through your window from outside in your yard, or through apartment windows from far away with binoculars."

"And that earns bad Karma?"

"Yes."

"How significant is that type of bad Karma?"

"Well, compared to murdering somebody, not very significant. But if the peeping Tom does this over and over then he is accumulating more and more bad Karma."

"I guess that makes sense. So, how does bad Karma get paid for?"

"That is not a simple answer. A murderer will likely need to experience the horrors of being murdered in this or a future lifetime. I really cannot say how a peeping Tom would pay for those debts, but the more accumulated bad Karma a soul acquires the more difficulties in general the soul will be put through when incarnated in future lifetimes. Having said all of that, forgiveness is another factor in the world of Karma. Sincere kindness to others without expecting any rewards, like Dacque's Good-Samaritan activities, results in the accumulation of good Karma. This helps balance out accumulated bad Karma. Hopefully, that gives you the general picture, but I need to leave you now for some regeneration. You can bring the subject up again another time if you like. Bye for now, Sis," the spirit said and commenced to dematerialize.

"Bye."

35

Connie received an email from Eyeonthepast on Monday, confirming that her second regression session was scheduled for the upcoming Saturday at nine in the morning at the same location where her first one was held. Connie emailed Eye back immediately to confirm the details and more importantly to explain that she in particular on this occasion wished to uncover another significant incarnation that she experienced with the soul of Zianos. She also sent along the wording that Zianos had suggested to her and asked Eyeonthepast if all of this was considered appropriate instructions during a regression session. Connie was well aware that she would only receive fifty minutes of Eye's time and at the end of her session Eye would be packing up her belongings and running out the door to get to her next appointment. Connie was determined not to waste any of her valuable fifty minutes filling Eye in on exactly what she wished to accomplish during this second regression session. Eye replied and assured her that all of the instructions and procedures that she wished her to use in the regression session were indeed possible and would be followed.

Connie was excitedly waiting with Dacque and Dani for Eyeonthepast's arrival on Saturday morning at Dacque's apartment. Being Eye's first appointment of the day, she rang the buzzer at the front entrance of the apartment building at ten minutes before nine. After quick greetings all around, Dacque and Dani departed for their morning walk and Eyeonthepast had Connie stretched out in Dacque's easy chair, relaxing to the soothing sounds of Mother Nature as the clock chimed nine times.

Convinced that Connie progressed into a deep hypnotic state, Eyeonthepast continued her instructions. "I would like you to imagine that you are sliding down a gently sloping tunnel towards the light that you can see at the bottom. When you exit from the tunnel you will land in a past lifetime that you have not told me about previously but is one that your soul regards as very significant and is also one that you shared with the soul of Zianos, who you have told me about previously. Please let me know when you are out of the tunnel."

"I am out of the tunnel."

"Please tell me what you see or what you are doing."

"We are preparing to leave to return to our homes in the Egyptian lands."

"Where are you currently located?"

"In our temporary home in the Nubian lands."

"How long have you been away from your home in the Egyptian lands?"

"Over ten years."

"Why have you been away so long?"

"Our beloved High Priest Ra-Ta was banished from the Egyptian lands for breaking one of his own cardinal rules. A group of over two hundred supporters left with him and settled in the Nubian lands."

"Are you a relative of Ra-Ta's?"

"No, a supporter."

"What is your name?"

"Cleodona."

"Are you female?"

"Yes."

"How old are you?"

"Thirty-five."

"Do you have a family with you in the Nubian lands?"

"Yes."

"Tell me about your family."

"My husband is Dagestan. We have two daughters and one son."

"Could I have their names, please?"

"Our daughters are Raeodona and Paeodona. Our son is the youngest and his name is Tagestan."

"Do you have other relatives that are with you in the Nubian lands?"

"Yes."

"Please identify them and explain your relationships."

"Dagestan's brother and his family also came with us. His brother's name is Ragestan. His wife is Nandemondu. They have two daughters called Randemondu and Landemondu."

"Thank you. Are you happy to be returning to the Egyptian lands?"

"Oh yes. None of my own family came with us and it will be wonderful to see them again after all of these years."

"What are the names of your parents?"

"My father is Tagestan also. We named our son after him. My mother is Saraconteen and my younger brother is Sagestan."

"What will you do when you get back to the Egyptian lands after all of these years?"

"The messenger, who was sent from the Egyptian lands to beg Ra-Ta to return and to bring all of us with him, said that we would work in our same or similar positions as we had when we left and would also be supplied with homes similar to the ones we left if our old homes were occupied by others."

"That was very kind of the authorities back in the Egyptian lands."

"Yes, but we believe that King Araaraart was so desperate for Ra-Ta to accept his invitation to return that he made sure the rewards for returning were too beneficial to turn down."

"Why was Ra-Ta's returning so important to King Araaraart?"

"Ra-Ta is a genius and a natural leader. He performed miracles working with the various ethnic groups that inhabited our area from many different lands. Ra-Ta was the social and economic leader under King Araaraart and transformed our surrounding area from a state of disorganized chaos into unprecedented prosperity. His long-term plans for us seemed too farfetched for many of the locals to accept at first, but he proved without a doubt that his dream for a perfect society was more than just a dream. After Ra-Ta was banished from the Egyptian lands chaos slowly seeped back into their system. No one else seemed to have the abilities and insight to maintain the momentum of progress after Ra-Ta was gone."

"That is very interesting. If Ra-Ta was so important to the country, why was he banished in the first place?"

"That is a good question and it turned out without a doubt that it was the wrong decision for the good of the country. There was some backroom manipulation afoot perpetrated by some of his detractors. Part of Ra-Ta's plan for a perfect society was to place people into occupations that they were best suited for. It also included breeding the more intelligent people to each other to produce a society of super intellectual leaders whose descendants would continue our progress for generations to come. The plan included a man only having one woman or wife. Ra-Ta had a wife and family but some of his detractors conceived a plan to bring him down and rounded up the most beautiful maiden they could find to entice him to be unfaithful. Unfortunately, their plan worked, and the maiden became pregnant giving the detractors the ammunition that they needed to demand that Ra-Ta be executed for his sins. His friend and admirer, King Araaraart, would not hear of that but to appease the detractors decided that Ra-Ta should be banished from the kingdom as his punishment."

"That is so interesting, but it is time for us to move on. I would like you to look around at the family members and close friends that you had in that lifetime in the Nubian and Egyptian lands and tell me if you can identify any of them that are also a part of your current lifetime here in Anywhere. If so, please give their names and relationships in both lifetimes."

"My husband Dagestan is the soul of Zianos. Our daughter Paeodona is my daughter Cammi today. Our son Tagestan is today my husband Carson. My brother-in-law Ragestan is Dacque LaRose. My mother Saraconteen is again my mother, Roberta Gannon. My brother Sagestan is my current father, Carman Gannon."

Eyeonthepast quickly inserted a new CD in her CD player.

"Thank you, Cleodona. I would like you now to imagine that you are once again back in the gently downward sloping tunnel sliding along slowly towards the light at the bottom. When you exit from the tunnel you will land in a past lifetime that is significant to your current lifetime but one that you have not already told me about. Please let me know when you are out of the tunnel."

"I am out of the tunnel."

"Please let me know what you see or what you are doing."

"I can't find my husband or the boys," Connie screamed. "Have you seen them? I have to find them," she continued, and began to climb out of Dacque's easy chair.

Eyeonthepast quickly placed the palms of her hands on Connie's shoulders and prevented her from standing up. "It's okay. Everything is going to be okay," she said in a soothing voice.

"Where are my boys? My husband? Have you seen them?" Connie continued to scream.

"It is going to be okay. Try and calm down and tell me what happened."

Connie settled back against the chair, gasping for air. She began to sob. "I can't find them. I can't find them. I have looked everywhere that I can go but there is so much destruction, so much rubble, that it is impossible to proceed very far."

"What caused the destruction?"

"A big earthquake."

"Where are you now?"

"In the street near what is left of our home. I have to find my husband and boys. Do you know where they are?"

"No, but I am sure they are safe wherever they are. You need to calm down."

Connie was silent but continued to take long, deep breaths. "The entire town appears to be destroyed. There is rubble everywhere. Hardly anybody is out in the streets."

"What is the name of your town?"

"Sant'Angelo dei Lombardi."

"I am not familiar with that name. Where is it located?"

"In Italy. In the south of Italy. In the mountains."

"Thank you. What year is it?"

"1694."

"What is your name?"

"Adelina."

"What is your husband's name?"

"Alberto."

"And the names of your boys?"

"Bernardo and Benedetto."

"Those are lovely names." Eyeonthepast wanted to ask more questions about the earthquake but was fearful of upsetting

Adelina again now that she had become somewhat calmed down. "How are you feeling now?"

"Better, thank you."

"Oh, that's good."

"Have you always lived in Sant'Angelo dei Lombardi?"

"No. I was born in the nearby town of Torella dei Lombardi and raised there. Alberto's family lived here in Sant'Angelo dei Lombardi. My father arranged our marriage with Alberto's father, and I moved here of course. Our families are related way back."

"How old are you, Adelina?"

"Thirty."

"How old is Alberto?"

"Thirty-three."

"And the boys?"

"Bernardo is eight and Benedetto is six."

"What does Alberto do for a living?"

"He is a cook in the Lombard Castle."

"Oh, that sounds like a good job. Does he like working in the castle?"

"Most of the time. When there are large gatherings he has to remain there for days and he does not enjoy that. He is compensated for this with time off when there is little activity at the castle."

Eyeonthepast decided that the smart move here was to avoid any further questions concerning the earthquake and the destruction of lives and buildings that resulted. She reasoned that if Cancan wanted further information from this lifetime, she could request it in a later regression session. "I would like you to now look around at your relatives and close friends in Sant'Angelo dei Lombardi and Torella dei Lombardi and tell me if any of them are incarnated with you again in your current lifetime. If any of them are, please identify them in both lifetimes and indicate their relationships to you."

"Angelo is again my husband, Carson Cantland. Bernardo is Carson's father Carl Cantland. Benedetto is my father Carman Gannon."

"Thank you for that information." Eye glanced at her watch. Ten minutes to ten. One of those days, she thought to herself. No time to investigate a third lifetime. "I am now going to slowly bring you out of your hypnotic trance state. I will count down from ten to one and when I reach the word one you will wake up feeling refreshed and remember most of the information that you shared with me today. Ten… nine… eight, you are beginning to wake up. Seven… six… five… four, you are now beginning to become aware of your surroundings. Three… two… one! Wake up!"

Connie stretched her arms in the air and stared at Eyeonthepast. "Did I dream some of that or was it as scary as I think it was?"

"I am pretty sure you relived a real experience from both lifetimes today. I stopped after two because I was running short on time and I did not want to rush out the door on you today after squeezing in a third lifetime. How are you feeling?"

"My heart feels like it is pounding a mile a minute."

"Have you had any heart problems?"

"No."

"Good. You should be alright then. Just sit there and relax for a few minutes or if you prefer, get up and walk around the apartment a bit while I gather up my things." Eye rounded up her belongings while Connie circled the apartment. "Here are the two CDs from today's session. Number one is quite fascinating, and I am sure you will enjoy listening to it. I would not recommend that you listen to number two for quite some time. You probably recall how upset you were at the beginning?"

"I remember."

"How do you feel now?"

"Much better, thank you. I'll be fine."

"Good. Are you going to call Dani or just go home?"

"I thought we were supposed to use our aliases within the group?"

"Some of us who have been around for a while get to know each other and the alias rule is basically only in place to make sure an inappropriate individual does not sneak into our little community. You obviously know both Dacque and Dani and they know you so we can dispense with the aliases unless others are around."

"I understand. Thank you for doing today's session for me. I will call Dani's cell number because Dacque does not own a cell phone."

Eyeonthepast smiled. "Some folks just cannot be modernized. You are welcome. See you around," Eye said and headed for the door.

36

Dacque and Dani were back at Dacque's apartment within ten minutes of receiving Connie's telephone call. Dani immediately noticed that Connie was as white as a sheet. "Oh, oh, what happened?"

Connie expelled a deep sigh as she fought back another bout of tears. "The first incarnation that I uncovered was the one that I requested with the soul of Zianos. It even turned out to also be the one with Dacque from the time of this Ra-Ta character, back in the early Egyptian days. I provided an amazing amount of interesting information that I am sure Dacque will enjoy hearing one of these days. The second incarnation I uncovered was the real shocker. It had me screaming and sobbing and Eyeonthepast needed to work her magic to keep me calm to get through it."

"On my," Dani declared. "You don't have to talk about it, you know?"

"I know. I cannot tell you much anyway as apparently neither of you were part of that incarnation. It took place back in 1694 in the mountains of southern Italy. There was a major earthquake, and our town was reduced to rubble. Somehow, I survived, apparently not seriously hurt, and I was seeking my husband and two sons but could not go very far through the rubble."

"Okay, that's enough," Dacque interrupted. "Now and then we uncover an unfortunate incident, and it is probably in our best interests to try to file it in a back corner of our memories for a while. Months down the road we may get up the courage to listen to that CD and try to figure out why our soul presented it to us at that time."

"Why would any soul think that a past lifetime that included the suffering from a major earthquake be significant to this lifetime?" Dani asked.

"Good question. All I can really say is that it may have come up as significant because of the people from this lifetime that Connie shared that life with. Did you identify anyone, Connie?"

"Actually, yes. A number of people close to us today. Well, my friends, I guess I had better head off home to my current family. I know Carson will be quite curious to hear how this morning went. Oh, before I forget, Dacque, Cammi has been invited over to a little friend's house this afternoon so she will not be around for story time today."

Dacque smiled. "Good for her. I am going to pick Mary up soon for our usual Saturday get together. She does enjoy her visits with your family, but I am sure we will find something interesting we can do for a few hours before I need to return her back home. She has another date with the same boy as two weeks ago."

"Cool. Are you still okay with Carson holding his second session with Eye here a week from now?"

"Of course."

"Great. Thank you again for putting up with us so often."

"It is my pleasure, trust me."

37

Connie had more up her sleeve than she let on to Dacque and Dani. She possessed ample time to sort out her options before Cammi departed for her little friend's place for the afternoon. With Cammi underfoot, when she returned home from her tumultuous adventure at Dacque's, she advised Carson that she would bring him up to date when they were alone for the afternoon.

Connie surprised Carson after lunch when she advised him that he was dropping Cammi off at her friend's for the afternoon instead of her. He offered no protest because he could tell from her unusual sullenness that there was something bothering her.

As soon as Cammi and Carson departed for Cammi's friend's house, Connie headed for Cammi's room. She sat on the side of her daughter's bed instead of her usual spot on the floor. "Hello Zianos. If you are here, please do not begin to materialize. I need to talk to you first and I do not want you using up your energy too soon today. If you can let me know in some way that you are here listening to me while only using a minimum of your energy, please do so." The fan over Cammi's bed turned on.

"Hey, that works. Thank you. Were you at Dacque's apartment this morning for my regression session? If yes, let me know." The fan slowed down and stopped. "I know that it is against the rules of our reincarnation group to let Carson listen to my CD from the Ra-Ta incarnation that I shared with you and Dacque, without Carson first uncovering that incarnation in his own regression session, but because he was there with us and the CD contains so much information, I would like him to listen to it today. I will be honest with you. There is a second reason as well. I really do not want him to have his second regression session next Saturday as scheduled because he might also uncover our incarnation in Italy that upset me so much today. I know there is a good possibility that he did not survive the earthquake and I really do not want to confirm that any time soon. Do you understand all of that?" The fan started up again.

"Good. I assume you will be there with us when I play the Ra-Ta CD for Carson in the living room but if you remain invisible, we will have more time to talk to you later. I will tell Carson that you are with us but at my request you are invisible to preserve your energy. We also have a fan over the dining room table, as you know, that you can use to communicate with us the same way you and I are doing right now. Are you okay with all of that?" The fan slowed down and stopped. "Thank you. See you, err, well not exactly, but you know what I mean, in the living room," Connie said and stood up to leave.

Connie paced circles around the living room floor until she heard Carson's car pull into the driveway and then she sat down. She found some parts of her plan disturbing but she was pretty sure she had it mapped out the best way she possibly could.

Carson joined her in the living room. "Okay, what is going on that you have not told me?"

Connie grinned. "Obvious, was it?"

"Oh yes. Out with it."

Connie sighed. "Okay, here goes. The first incarnation that I uncovered was the one I requested where I was with the soul of Zianos another time. It also happened to be the one with Dacque and that fellow called Ra-Ta you have heard us mention a few times. The information I provided on that lifetime is incredible. You were there with us also and will probably uncover that lifetime in your next regression session. But I would like you to listen to my CD now ahead of time. You will be amazed at what you hear."

"Isn't that against the rules?"

"Yes, but I won't tell anyone if you don't tell anyone, okay?"

Carson laughed. He was delighted to see that his beautiful wife was feeling more relaxed as they conversed. "Okay. It's a deal."

"Good. There is more. When you drove Cammi to her friend's house I headed for her bedroom to see if Zianos was around, and he was. I specifically asked him not to materialize so he could preserve his energy, to talk to us later, but instead to come up with a way of communicating with me which did not deplete his energy very much. He is here with us now to listen to my first CD along with us, even though he was at Dacque's apartment with me this morning during the regression session, so he knows every word that is on it. If you are here Zianos, show Carson your talking machine." The fan over the dining room table commenced to whirl.

"How did he do that?"

"I don't know. I never bothered to ask him. I was more concerned with important things than worrying about how it works. All we need to do is ask the question in the proper manner and he will respond to it. If that is correct Zianos, answer with the fan." The fan began to slow down and come to a stop.

"I love it. Is there anything else?"

"First things first. I want you to listen to the Ra-Ta CD now, okay?"

"Give it a spin."

Connie walked over to her CD player and started the CD. They both listened attentively and silently throughout the entire recording.

"You were not kidding when you said that it contained an amazing amount of information. There is no way I will remember all of that, but we have the CD and can play it as often as we like."

"Definitely. So, do you have any questions that you would like to ask me or Zianos?"

Carson contemplated in silence for a minute. "I probably do not remember half of what I heard but you were marvelously clear in your explanations for Eyeonthepast. I actually cannot think of one question at this time, but I am definitely going to listen to it a number of times before I have my session next Saturday."

"Great. That brings us to the next item on my list. I do not think you should have your next regression session next Saturday, but instead postpone it for a while."

"Did I hear that right? What's going on?"

"There was a problem with the second incarnation that I spoke about this morning. It was from back a few centuries in Europe and my town was hit with a devastating earthquake pretty much wiping out the town, I assume. I somehow survived the quake and started my narrative for Eyeonthepast screaming and sobbing, as I watched myself searching for my husband and children and could not get very far through the rubble. Eye literally had to hold me in the chair when I tried to climb out and search for them. She worked diligently to calm me down so we could gather some information on that incarnation, but she discretely avoided asking me certain questions about the survival of my family members. You were one of my family members and I am a long way from ready to discover that you did not survive the earthquake. If you have a second regression session you may also uncover that incarnation with the earthquake and discover who did or did not survive in our family. As I said, I am in no frame of mind to hear the answer to that question so please postpone your second regression session, indefinitely."

By the time Connie completed her pleading it was obvious to Carson that she was one step away from hysterical. "Relax, honey. It is definitely, indefinitely postponed."

"Thank you," Connie whispered and burst into tears.

Carson stood up and reached over for Connie, pulling her up and into his comforting arms where she sobbed on his shoulder for three of four minutes. When the shower trickled to a stop Connie went to retrieve some tissues from the dining room and headed for the kitchen to clear her nasal passages. Carson sat down and waited. A few minutes later she reappeared and walked towards the living room, stopping at the corner of the dining room table. "You are welcome to listen to the second CD if you like but I will not listen to it. I will go outside for a walk, instead. Zianos, does Carson really need to listen to the second CD. If you think he should listen to it now, please turn the fan on."

Both of them stared at the fan that remained asleep.

"Zianos has been patiently hanging out with me, and then us, for quite a while now this afternoon, and we have not even invited him to materialize," Connie said. "As you can tell, I have had quite a day of it, and I do not really have any more questions for him today. Do you have questions for him?"

Carson contemplated for a few seconds. "No, not really."

"Well, Zianos, my dear twin brother, I thank you immensely

for your assistance throughout my struggles this afternoon. You were even able to preserve most of your energy to pop off somewhere else where you may also be needed."

"You're welcome," a soft voice said and then the room fell silent.

38

The weeks whirled by and transformed into months. The Cantland household settled into a semblance of normality as the Holiday season approached. On a chilly, Thursday late afternoon Connie waited excitedly in the living room for her delayed husband to arrive for dinner. Cammi was playing in her bedroom while Connie had their dinner warming on the stove. When she heard Carson's car in the driveway, she hopped up off of the sofa and hurried out to the foyer to wait for him.

"Well, how did it go today?" he eagerly asked.

"We are definitely pregnant," a smiling Connie declared and rushed into his open arms for a passionate embrace.

No one was there to see the soul of Zianos happy-dancing all around the dining room, singing silently to himself: *I finally get to join my family! I finally get to join my family!*

Dear reader,

We hope you enjoyed reading *Invisible Friends*. Please take a moment to leave a review, even if it's a short one. Your opinion is important to us.

Discover more books by Doug Simpson at https://www.nextchapter.pub/authors/doug-simpson

Want to know when one of our books is free or discounted? Join the newsletter at http://eepurl.com/bqqB3H

Best regards,

Doug Simpson and the Next Chapter Team

Manufactured by Amazon.ca
Bolton, ON